SILENT DREAMS

Lord Bless You
"Denise"

Thanks

George Wall Jr
"Dollar Bill"
08/10/2012

SILENT DREAMS

☽

George Washington

aka Dollar Bill

Copyright © 2006 George Washington
All rights reserved.
ISBN 978-1-4243-2918-2

Mary Elizabeth Washington
Born: 1892
Went to a better life: 1968

I would like to dedicate this book to my Grandmother Mrs. Mary E. Washington who was, and still is, an inspiration in my life. While I was young she taught me a lot of wisdom. She taught me much about life and what I may expect. The biggest thing she taught me was to not worry, God is in control. Tomorrow is never promised, so enjoy today. She was an inspiration to everyone who met her, and yes, she was one of God's angels. I'll always love you, Grandmother. Thanks for your love and compassion.

Your Grandson,
George Washington

SILENT DREAMS

CHAPTER 1

Kannapolis, City of Looms. A small town twenty miles north of Charlotte, North Carolina, is where our story takes places. I am Kevin Cole and I grew up here years ago. As I narrate parts of this story, I want you to let your mind place you in our little city and feel what we felt growing up there. Think of growing up in a town where ninety percent of the time you feel nothing but peace. The other ten percent you let the adults worry about. Enough meditating, back to our story and the reason I love to come home.

It is a mill town—that's how the name evolved. The local cotton mill built the town. A mill that uses cotton to make sheets, pillowcases, bedspreads, towels and more. That's where the phase "City of Looms" originated, thus Kannapolis was born.

The mill provides a good life for the people in the area. It's a rural city because of the growth it's going through, but to me it will always be country.

I love the peace and joy in this town plus the easy living it seems to have. Turning off the highway to Kannapolis, I started to feel the ease. Driving up Route 29—known as Cannon Boulevard—the time seemed to slow down. Landscapes started to change, no more buildings to steal your sunlight or smog to choke your life away, like you have in the big cities. As I passed each home the yards were big, back and front. Trees were on every corner and flowers graced the land. Upon passing a K-mart, it was alone on a lot. In big cities you see building on top of building, but in Kannapolis every store has its own space.

A funeral passed on the left and all the traffic on both sides of the highway came to a standstill. As I drove on up the highway I couldn't help but notice there were fruit stands on both sides of the road. Restaurants and small stores were mixed in with the houses as well. One of the larger stores had a little circus on its lot. It was as if I were entering a new world or new way of life, the kind most of us were trying to forget about.

Suddenly I made a right turn off the highway up on a bridge to First Street. As I drove on slowly, there was a high school located on the right (A.L. Brown High), it looked peaceful also. Then I made a left behind the school, drove up Elm Street and stopped. As I looked to my left I could see George Washington Carver, the elementary school I use to attend. I drove on and crossed over another street to finally reach my destination. There I entered the neighborhood where John Fields lives; it seemed to get even more peaceful. I wound down a dirt road that had a dead end; John's house was located on the right.

John Fields, a young black male standing about four feet eleven inches tall, smiles gently as he looked at the early morning sunlight. His coffee-black complexion shone like gold as the sun hit his skin. His eyes were dark brown, with a deep look; his friends call him "The Thinker."

John stood casually on the porch, wearing blue jeans with a green checkered shirt and an old ball cap that one of his uncles had given him from when he played in the Old Negro Baseball League. John wore this cap all the time; it was his good luck charm. Although he didn't believe in luck that much, he wore it because his favorite uncle had given it to him. His faith was what he believed in the most.

John loved the woods; it brought him peace and tranquility. While in the woods he enjoyed life. While there he loved to sit and look at the water. There is a small stream that flowed from one end of the town to the other, and then emptied into a beautiful lake, which provided water to the next town. The stream water was so clear it looked as if it should be bottled. This is where John found the most peace.

There were all types of creatures using this stream. But when it rained the creek rose quickly, creating danger for every person or creature in the area, but soon it was back to normal and life resumed. Next to its beauty, another reason that John loved the woods was all of his friends played there all day long. Also while in the woods he found an area he called his special place. This was where he spent most his time thinking, writing poems and enjoying the wild life. This was something his grandmother taught him. She told him to "find you a place quiet to think and talk to GOD."

As I looked around the neighborhood, everyone seemed to be so relaxed. Most of the male adults got off work and gathered on a particular porch to wind down. All the kids found their individual groups to play with and the pets ran free, like creatures of the wild. Yes, let's not forget mom. The mothers started getting their families' dinners ready.

This setting reminded me of a day long ago. One day John and his friends were building cars of wood. John's parents had bought him a pretty red wagon for Christmas that he had taken the wheels from to put on their wooden car. All the kids would do this, and then they would have a race.

"Come on John," yelled Roosevelt, one of his friends, as they ran to the start line. John was the smallest on his team so he got to ride. As they lined up for the start of the race, the boys made sounds like cars revving their engines. John's team (Team Three) had never lost a race.

Bernard gave the command to start the race. "Are you ready? Team three, are you ready to start?"

"Yes we are," they replied.

Bernard yelled out the commands, "Ready, set, go!" He dropped the green flag and the race was on.

The first leg of the race was a one-hundred-yard

straightaway, it was a sprint. Afterwards you hit dead man's curve, a forty-five-degree turn. The people in the neighborhood named it that because there was an accident there every three or four years in which someone got killed in an automobile. Usually they were drinking alcohol and driving. That doesn't mix.

Once the boys rounded the curve it was downhill for another one hundred yards, then into another small curve that was not as bad as the first. Once you made it out of this curve there were only fifty yards to the finish line.

Roosevelt and Mike pushed John as fast as they could. All the teams were even at the fifty-yard mark, where John's team started to push ahead. Once they pulled ahead of the other teams they knew this race was going to be their toughest yet. Usually they made a late charge, but this time they were leading too early.

Still, they pushed as hard as they could. Every team was coming up on dead man's curve—the toughest curve on the course. As Team Three went into the curve another team pulled even. John had to go wide and almost slid in the ditch. "John, take it easy up there and keep us on the road," yelled Mike.

Suddenly, Team Three's car started to shake really badly.

"What's going on?" yelled Roosevelt.

"I don't know," said John, "but it doesn't sound good." Then, all of a sudden, one of the steering mechanisms came loose. They were only made from clothes hangers and nailed to the front end, but usually they held well.

"Fellows, we have a problem," yelled John.

"What type of problem?" they yelled back.

"I have no controls."

"Put your feet on the front and steer," replied Mike.

"Okay, it's working," yelled John.

Then the wheels turned sharply to the left and John ran off the road into the ditch. The curve was too much to overcome.

"Are you hurt, little man?" asked his teammates as they helped him up.

"I am fine, but we lost," said John.

"That's okay, as long as you're not hurt," said Mike.

"Yes, don't worry, we can race them another day," replied Roosevelt.

They both gave John a big hug and the three boys walked off. John learned how to lose that day, but he also found out that his friends really cared about him, and that meant a lot.

As the sun started to set on this little town, people came out and began to relax on their porches and enjoyed the evening. Unlike the city, you could hear the creatures of the night and count every star in the sky. At last, the town was at rest.

Three weeks later, summer arrived in Kannapolis. The flowers were so beautiful and had the sweetest fragrance in the world. Most people grew their own gardens so they could have fresh vegetables all summer. Of course, there were fruit stands all over the place. People who owned their own farms added more beauty to this town.

Every year they would sell their products locally and to the surrounding towns.

Although Kannapolis was a wonderful place to live, it was not the town itself that most parents were concerned about. They wanted their kids to experience new jobs, new areas, and not just settle for working in the mill. Although the mill was a great means of earning a living, they wanted their children to go to college and be more successful. Parents would tell their children to travel the world, and then if they wanted to, to return to Kannapolis. Cities in the USA were changing, and so were the people, but Kannapolis would stay the same throughout time thanks to the people who lived there.

John and his friends walked through the neighborhood one day and decided to go to the other side of town. They had no idea how much this decision was going to change their lives. As they passed by a restaurant they saw a sign on the door which read WHITES ONLY. The meaning was white people only were allowed enter through that door.

The sign disturbed John badly. Although he was only twelve years old, he was beginning to see the ways of the world.

He didn't like what he read. He started for the door, but his friends stopped him, saying, "You can't go in that door, it's for white people only."

John said, "Well, I don't believe that's right, and I refuse to listen."

"We're supposed to use the back door," said another friend.

"No, John, don't do it man," they all yelled.

"Why?" asked John.

"Because those people are not nice," yelled Bill.

"They yell racial names at us, and use words that are unkind," said another friend.

"How do you know they hate us?" asked John?

"You know what our parents told us about the hanging and lynching of our people in the old days? Well, that still takes place," said Keith.

"Our parents told us what they used to do to them years ago, and I am sure yours have told you, John," said one of his friends.

"That was years ago," replied John. "We can't keep living in the past. Why can't we go in any door we choose?" he said.

"Well, I am not afraid, so I am going in. Anyway, we can't always be afraid."

"No, John, please don't," begged his friends as he walked on.

As he approached the doorway of the restaurant a warm calmness came over him. It was like a voice saying *You're doing the right thing. Brave young man, have faith and let your heart guide you.*

He opened the door slowly and walked in. Once inside he looked around. He was a little afraid, but determined to overcome his fear, so he kept on walking.

Everyone in the restaurant was white. They all began to look at him as if he didn't belong. They began to murmur among themselves, and one of the men spoke to John.

"Boy, you're not supposed to come in that door."

John stopped because they were looking at him strangely. Then one of the weirdest things happened. The owner of the restaurant came from behind the counter and walked slowly toward John.

As she approached him the room became very silent. She looked at John and smiled. He smiled back and said, "Hello."

"Hello, little fellow, what's your name?"

"My name is John Fields."

He said it in such an authoritative voice that afterward you could hear a pin drop. The owner, Mrs. Betty Hugging, was very impressed and told him so.

"With a strong voice like that I feel you will be a great leader one day."

She gave him a big hug and looked around.

"Everyone, this is John Fields, and he is my new friend."

They all said hello and clapped their hands. "Come with me," she said, and took John to the counter. As he sat down his friends were outside looking in through the window, afraid but glad to see the brave heart of their friend.

"What is your favorite pie?"

"Apple," said John.

"Would you like milk?"

"Yes ma'am."

"You're the first Colored person to every come through that door, and I am proud of you."

"Ma'am, it is okay to say 'Black' person. People my age don't like the phrase 'Colored person'."

"Well, I have a lot of black friends," she said, "and I love them all."

As the owner talked, John could feel her pain. She didn't like the sign on the door, but the government made her place it there. When he left she took the sign off the door and told John to come back anytime and bring his friends.

John had made a very special friend, a friend for life. The signs on all the businesses started to come down later that year. The government passed a law prohibiting discrimination to any race, creed or color. Thus by believing in something so strongly, John and millions of people got rights by way of the Discrimination Act of 1968.

One month later John sats at a table where his grandmother filled him with wisdom. Everyday he ran over to her house after school. She was a very special lady. His grandma was a Christian, and was loved by everyone in the community. Her hair was long, with salt and pepper color. John looked at her as an angel.

Her name was Mary Elizabeth Fields. In her seventies, she enjoyed life to the fullest, because she didn't have a worry in the world. She had faith in GOD, and knew she would be going home to be with HIM one day.

"Grandmother, you're the best friend in the whole world and I never want to lose you."

"Now, son," she said, "one day I'll be going home to be with the Lord."

"But why do you have to leave?"

"We all have to leave one day, for as sure as you're born

in this life, you must die, and my time is near. You just remember, I will always be with you," she replied.

In a way, John knew what his grandmother was getting him ready for, and he didn't want to think of that. He would be ready, although all of the wisdom that he learned still wouldn't lessen the pain he would feel.

One day John was visiting her, and she told him to go out and gather his friends.

"Tell them to bring their BB Rifles."

John did as he was told. He went to all of his friends' houses and asked them to come with him with their BB Rifles. As they started for his grandmother's house, Steve, Kevin, Will, Otis, Don, Kirk, Reggie, Bernard and Roosevelt were with him. They didn't know what he wanted, but when he said that his grandmother sent for them, they all began to run as fast as they could because they all loved her dearly.

As they ran into the yard, their little faces were filled with excitement. Mrs. Fields was sitting on the porch in her favorite rocking chair. Her children had purchased it for her years ago.

"Here are all my friends, Grandmother," said John.

"Now I want all of you to go out and hunt up a mess of birds," said Mrs. Fields.

In those days it was socially acceptable for people to eat birds, squirrels and rabbits that they hunted for a meal. Now people feel it's wrong to hunt the animals that GOD placed here for us to eat.

Mrs. Fields said, "Don't kill any red or black ones. The

red birds are our state symbol, and black birds have purple stomachs and are not good to eat. When you return, I'll make a great feast. All of you have been so good, John, you deserve a reward and this is my way of giving just that," she replied.

So they all left and went into the woods looking for birds, but only for the ones that Mrs. Fields had told them to kill. Once they reached the edge of the woods, they didn't have to look far. The trees were suddenly full of birds. They were the most beautiful birds that the boys had ever seen.

"Where did they come from, John?" asked Reggie.

"I don't know, but they are here for us, I think," he replied. They began shooting the birds."

They had never seen anything like it—the birds would not even fly. There were hundreds of birds on every tree. The boys were just shooting them, one by one. It seemed like the birds just appeared out of nowhere.

One of the boys, whose name was Kevin, didn't want the other boys to kill birds; not because it was too easy, but because he thought it was wrong and cruel. He tried to scare the birds away, but they wouldn't leave. It was meant to be. John's grandmother had a feast planned and the Lord gave us the birds. It must be mean chin that this was the first and last time the boys had seen these types of birds, so God had to have placed them there. They collected eleven bags of birds and headed back for John's grandmother's house, where she was sitting on her porch.

I will never forget that old house. It stood so beautiful,

like a castle in the sky. As the boys ran up to the porch John said, "Look, Grandmother, we have lots of birds."

She gave John a big hug and lifted him up. The smile on her face was one that John framed in his mind forever, for it was the last time that he saw her so happy.

"Now, young fellows, sit down here and pick the feathers off the best you can, and I'll get things started in the kitchen."

John's grandma was the best cook in the whole world. Everyone liked her cooking. While in the kitchen, she would always sing to relax. There was one song that she song the most: "Oh How I Love Jesus." And that she did.

When they finished cleaning the birds, John went and told her to let her know. "Y'all wait out on the porch and I will call you once it is ready."

While waiting for her to get the "feast" ready, John remembered when she saved his brother's life. He had cut his wrist badly, and the two boys ran inside the house to tell her. Everyone was scared and crying, but she kept calm and said, "Go find me some spider webs." John did so, and she grabbed her Bible off the shelf, opened it to a verse, and placed the web on his brother's wrist.

It was a miracle, for as she read the verse, the blood just stopped, and the verse she read stuck in John's head: believe in god and all things are possible. Yes, his grandmother was an instrument of GOD. She believed and put all her faith in him.

It seemed as though an hour had passed.

"John."

"Yes, Grandma?"

"Bring in your friends."

As the boys entered the kitchen they saw a meal fit for a king. The food placed an aroma in the house that they would never forget. John's grandmother said, "This is for my little Prince and his friends."

The table looked so elegant. There were four beautiful cooked pans of birds, roasted to a golden brown. Two pots had corn on the cob, boiling fresh. A pot of fresh green beans that John's grandmother took out of her garden yesterday stewed lightly on the stove. On top of all that, she cooked three pans of biscuits and all the tea the boys wanted to drink was there. "John," said his grandmother, "I have your favorite pie in the window, cooling." Yes, three apple pies were waiting on them and John would save room.

They ate until they couldn't eat anymore; the boys had joy that day. They thanked GOD and his grandmother for that. John's friends thanked her and told her that she was the best. When they went outside, Reggie went up to John and said, "John, you have the greatest grandmother in the whole world." He knew that, she had always been like that, for she was John's best friend.

Let it be said that Mrs. Elizabeth Fields was the backbone of their family. She was a leader in church and made sure that everyone in the family was good. At her house, she did it all; she was a strong woman. She cooked three meals a day, and she cleaned house and never complained about anything. Her family tried to get her to take it easy, but that's just how she was. She used to love to make quilts all year round. She made the best pies in the world. When John's grandmother talked, everyone listened. She was a very special lady, but her faith in God was what drew John so near. She taught him about God and the love of life.

This was the last winter John's grandmother saw. That spring, she took ill. John's dad and mom brought the family all together in the house. The kids knew it was something serious, because their dad had never had a tear in his eyes before. John's mom told them the news.

"We are going over to Grandmother's house. She is ill and she wants you all there."

As they started to leave for their grandmother's home, it seemed as though the path they walked through three or four times a day was very long, like a dream that would never end.

Finally, they came out of the woods. John could see her house. He didn't want to go because he knew what was wrong. His dad said, "Come on son. You know how much she loves you."

As they arrived at the house, everyone was so sad looking. All the kids were downstairs and the adults were upstairs. John had to go see her, so he asked his dad if he could.

"Yes, son, it's okay."

When he walked into the room, he could barely move. His grandmother told him to come closer and not be afraid.

"Remember I told you that I would be going home one day to be with God?"

"Yes, Grandmother."

"Well, the time has come for me to be with Him."

"I don't want you to go."

"Now, don't you worry, you just take care of yourself and be good. Remember the things I taught you and hold on to God's words." She went on to say, "Don't come to see me at the hospital."

"Why?" he asked.

"Because I want you to remember me the way I am. Not sick, but one of God's angels with a smile.

When I die, don't cry, just be happy. I'll be with God."

As John left the room, those words stuck in his head. That evening, while John was in the woods, in his special place, he began to write a poem about how his grandmother felt. It was a message from God he felt:

WHEN I DIE

When I die, don't cry or mourn
Just be happy that I am gone
Gone to a place where things are great.
Where you don't have to worry
Or don't have to wait
A place where things are white and pure,
Where you need no medicine
For there is nothing to cure
When I die, don't cry or mourn
Just be happy that I am gone.

> I am in God's care, so please don't fear
> And don't worry, for he holds me near
> But instead rejoice, be happy and smile.
> For that I also do.

John remembered how quiet the woods seemed that day as he walked home. They took his grandmother to the hospital that night. Everyone visited her. Friends and family went to visit her the entire week, but John would not join them. His mother asked if he wanted to go, but he told her that his grandmother told him not to, that she wanted him to remember her just the way she was. She was going to be with God and for John to be happy.

John will never forget March 16, a Friday morning. Every adult was getting in his or her car to leave for the hospital again. The minister was at the house getting them altogether; all the older kids were keeping the younger kids quiet. John remembered standing in the kitchen with his brother and a few cousins, when a warm wind gently blew over his face. It felt as if he was being lifted up. It reminded him of the way his grandmother used to hug him.

Then he heard a voice speak to him.

"John, tell everyone I love them and don't worry about me. John, I will always be with you. Whenever the wind blows, think of me hugging you. I love you. Remember, always keep your faith and believe in God. Goodbye."

At that point, John turned to his brother and cousins and said, "Grandmother just died."

His brother said, "Shut up."

"I said it's the truth, and she told me to tell all of you that she loves you," John said.

His brother was very upset and started to fight with John. A cousin pulled them apart. Everyone thought that John was crazy.

Thirty seconds later, the telephone rang. John's uncle answered it. It was the doctor. "Tell your family to take their time, Mrs. Fields just passed."

At that point, they all looked at John, because this was a gift that his grandmother had. She had the wisdom; John guessed it was inside of him and it would forever make him different from the rest of his family.

They prepared for her funeral. All loved her and they showed her. She had one of the largest funerals in the history of Kannapolis. People of all races came from miles around to say goodbye to a great saint. John didn't know that she had touched so many people, but through God she had. As the minister started to speak about his grandmother, he couldn't help but wonder about the things she had taught him. Always truth in God, and show your love to others as through his eyes.

She was missed by all but not forgotten. Mrs. Fields was loved by all and as the minister asked if there was anyone who would love to make comments about his grandmother, John jumped up and began to sing. He could not stop singing either. "All that I am and all that I use to be; Truly Committed," was the song he sang. He didn't want to get up, but a force pushed him up. Yes, it was the Holy Spirit at work and he was glad.

When the minister finished preaching, they headed for the burial site. It was raining lightly and a beautiful rainbow formed. John was told that if it rained during a funeral, that an angel was going to heaven. Yes, she was going home to be with the Lord. As they left the church, the choir walked and sang all the way to the gravesite.

It was a very happy moment. The joy that hit the people as they arrived at the burial site was great. Everyone started to sing and dance. If there was a tear, they were tears of joy. They sang, "We're going over yonder to be with the Lord." Everyone sang for an hour, it seemed, as they lowered her body into the ground.

At that point John knew it hit him—what Grandma was trying to teach him. Enjoy what little life you have on this earth; believe in God for there is a more beautiful life waiting on you. He loved her and one day he will be with her.

CHAPTER 2

My thoughts continued to flow one year later.

John Fields was awakened by the breaking of the day. John got dressed and raced out of his room. His mom stopped him. "John, you can't leave without eating your breakfast. Now sit down."

"Oh, Mom," he replied in gentle voice. "I want to get to the woods before the sun comes up. I love that part of the day."

"I know, son, but I love keeping you strong, so that you can go to the woods," replied his mom.

Rebecca Fields was the only one who got up before John. She got breakfast ready everyday and took great care of the family. Mrs. Fields was a strong woman who was well liked in the community.

She was raising five kids and keeping them out of trouble. Yes, she had to be strong. Everyday their meals were ready, their clothes were pressed for school and the house was clean. Her husband knew that he had one of the best women in the world. Their love was very special. He was there if strong discipline needed to be applied, but she was the one who kept the family together.

John complained a little, but sat down to eat. When he finished, he ran out of the house calling, "Thanks, Mom." His dad came into the kitchen next.

"Hello, Dear. May I have some coffee?"

"Have a seat and I will get you some."

Larry Fields was a mill worker. He had a drinking problem, but worked hard for his family. "Did I hear the door?"

"Yes, Honey. That was John going out."

Larry sipped his coffee. "I hope he is not going into the those woods again."

"Now, Dear, when you were a little boy you loved the woods. He is the same as you were. You're still one of the best hunters around. Now be quiet and drink your coffee—after all, boys will be boys."

Larry Fields was very upset because he couldn't find a better job. Rebecca was constantly telling him, "Honey, we need to get a bigger house for the kids."

"Well," Larry said, "We'll have to save to get one."

"Ill get a job and help,", Rebecca replied.

"You're not going to get a job. I told you before; the kids need you here at home.Now just get it out of your head."

This argument took place all the time. This is what drove John to the woods initially, along with his dad's drinking. John, although young, was very wise and knew it was bad for his dad. Sometimes when Larry got drunk, he would take it out on the kids and Rebecca.

Thinking back in the past about Larry: One night about six months ago, Larry came home drunk and in a bad mood. "Honey, where are the kids, he asked?" Rebecca said, "You know they're in bed." "I heard you been out looking for work."Larry said."Yes," said Rebecca, "We have to do better."

At that point they started to fight. John was awakened by the noise. He ran into the room to help his mom, and his dad smacked him down. It was the first time that his dad had ever done anything like that before. John was small for his age, but didn't want his parents fighting anymore. He loved his dad as a son should, and knew he could break the argument by getting his dad to focus on him—and it worked.

As John ran out of the house, his dad grabbed his shotgun and began chasing him. "You come back here. Don't run from me," yelled Larry.

John yelled back, "No!" John had never talked back to his dad and this was the first time he had ever run from him before. He believed in the father, son, love and obedience. It hurt him bad to do what he did, and he hoped both God and his dad would forgive him.

The neighbors called the police. When they arrived, John's dad had a twelve-gauge shotgun. They knew Larry well and knew he was a good person. Even though he had a drinking problem, something must have really made him mad for him to chase his son with a gun.

"Give us the gun Larry," yelled the policeman.

"What is the matter with you, Mr. Fields?"

"Don't any of my kids talk back to me," Larry replied.

"Okay, Larry, just put the gun down," Officer James said.

Larry laid the gun down. The policeman asked John if he wanted to press charges, but John loved his dad and refused to do so.

That was the last time John's dad ever beat him or his mother. That night, Rebecca was mad and out of her head. She came into the living room where Larry had fallen asleep. He awakened with a knife at his throat.

"Dear! What are you doing, are you crazy?"

"If you touch me or my children again, I promise you won't see another day."

Larry's life changed after that. They say that near-death has away of waking some of us up, as it did for Larry. He had never seen his wife in that mood before and he never would touch them again. He also slowed down his drinking; Rebecca went out and got a job to help out.

Larry never hit his wife or kids again. It was as if he changed and became someone else. Rebecca found a friend to help out with the kids. It worked out great, so they started to save for that bigger house.

The day was calm when John arrived in the woods. The sun was so beautiful as it came from behind the trees. He was jogging along the path, when suddenly stillness fell in the air. All the creatures that were around froze. They knew someone or something was coming. There were two little squirrels still scurrying around and around a tree. John stopped to play with them, but frightened by the noise, they ran up the tree.

As they stopped and looked down the tree, there was a gentle little boy standing there. That was the storm they heard coming. John knelt down beside the tree. It was an act that one of his elderly friends taught him. Mr. James (they called him Buddy) used to tell him to fill the creatures with his heart. Become as humble as he could and they would learn to trust him.

So every day he tried this. Each day the squirrels would get closer and closer. One day they would eat out of his hands. A noise soon sent them back up the tree. John got up and continued on his way, thinking that one day they would trust him, one day.

As he went through the woods, John felt so free, but yet alone. He thought of a lot of things. The one thought that crossed his mind the most was his grandmother. He would talk to her all the time. While in second grade, he remembered writing her a poem that won second place in a contest. It was simple but sweet. He called it "Grandmother."

> Grandmother
> For all that work
> And all that sweat.
> What did she get?

The teacher loved it and John has been writing ever since.

Grandmother, he thought to himself, *I need a special friend like I had with you, but I know that no one could ever take your place.*

Although alone, John was at home in the woods. He loved to study books and enjoyed running, but most of all he loved to go to the woods. His brothers and sisters thought he was weird. John would often relax and write while he was alone in the woods. He would also look after the little creatures which lived there.

Every morning he made his way to his special place, free like the animals that lived there. However, this day his life would change forever.

Off at a distance, he noticed a little girl about his age walking and singing.

"Hi, how are you?" yelled John.

She was startled and didn't answer.

"Are you okay?" But she just ran out of the wood as fast as she could.

"Come back" yelled John, but she did not.

Now he was alone again. He began to play when some more boys arrived. Thus began life in the woods.

CHAPTER 3

The young lady's name was Sara Moright. She was a frail young black girl standing about four feet, nine inches tall. Her eyes were bright as an eastern star shining brightly in the night. Her skin was smooth as silk. She was a beautiful child with an angelic aura that seemed to surround her. Although she was only twelve years old, she was in some way very spiritually mature.

When she went to the woods, she would sit and think about God and how awesome He must be. She watched the birds take care of their babies, she marveled at the beautiful butterflies, and she loved the various wildflowers she came across in the area of the wood she called her "special thinking place." She also thought about the young man she came across unexpectedly.

Neither John nor Sara was aware that they both loved the woods and that the two of them had always found a kind of peace there that was hard to explain. They both visited the woods alone, so it was destiny that one day they would meet there.

Sara's family was a proud one. Her father was an engineer at the mill where Larry Fields worked. Her mom was a housewife. Their family was torn apart because her father was about to lose his job. Her father's name was Jesse Moright, and her mom's name was Betty. She also had a brother, William. Although her father had a good job, he brought it home. He also drank. This is what drove Sara to the woods. At least there, everything was peaceful and quiet.

One day her father came home in a real bad mood. He told his wife that another company was purchasing the mill, and he didn't know what was going to happen. "I might not have a job any day now. Do you hear me? I won't be able to support my family."

Betty told him, "Don't worry, God will take care of us."

Being a man of little faith, he didn't believe at first, but God has a way of turning people around.

Betty said, "Don't worry, dear. Please don't worry!"

"I try not to, but I love my family, and want to take care of you. I'm going for walk so I can calm down."

Then he left. It was raining, but he didn't let that stop him. Betty just stood there and cried.

Meanwhile, Sara and her brother were sitting on the stairway. They believed what their mom had said, that God would take care of them. That night, while in her room, Sara was thinking about the young boy. *I hope he will be in the woods tomorrow,* she thought to herself. *I hope he will be there.*

Sara never saw the young boy coming toward her as

she walked to her special place, but all of a sudden he was there. She believed he asked her a question, in a soft voice, but since she wasn't expecting anyone to be there, of course she was frightened and quickly ran as fast as she could out of the woods.

Still that night, as she lay on her bed, she thought about the encounter. The boy seemed different from most boys her age. In fact, she had never seen him around. He must have attended a different school than hers. Also, Sara hadn't been living here very long, so this was probably why she hadn't seen him before. She thought that he probably didn't mean to frighten her.

However, Sara thought, *next time, I won't run away.* For some strange reason, she couldn't wait until tomorrow. As she started to drift off to sleep she thought, *I know he'll be there tomorrow, and this time I won't be scared.* The night soon grew silent and all was asleep.

The next day it rained, and Sara felt an immediate sadness, but she wasn't sure why. After all, she just seen him and didn't even know him.

Meanwhile, John woke up thinking about the little, frail, frightened girl he encountered in his special place. He, too, stayed home and felt sadness. He had learned a lot from his grandmother, who had taught him things well beyond his twelve years, like missing people or compassion for people.

It rained for one hour and stopped. Sara went to the woods but John wasn't there. Meanwhile, John went to look for his little friend, but she was nowhere to be found.

They just missed each other. As she was leaving in one direction, he was just coming in from the other.

When Sara returned home her father was waiting. "I through I told you to stay out of those woods. This is the last time I will tell you."

He turned to his wife. "Honey, I'm going to work now. Do you want any thing?"

"Yes, dear, stop by the store when you come home and pick up some sugar," replied Mrs. Moright.

"Sara?"

"Yes, Mom?"

"Try not to be mad at your dad, he has a lot on his mind. He may be losing his job and plus he worries about you."

"Yes, Mom." Sara went to her room. With all the problems at home, the woods seemed so safe for her. Beside the beauty of the woods, it felt so great when she was out there with mother nature.

Meanwhile, John had settled in the woods and once more he looked for the girl. She was nowhere to be found. *Maybe she'll be down later,* he thought to himself.

John always did the same things to get settled in the woods. He would cross over the creek on a water pipe that was about fourteen inches across. He and the boys used to see who could knock the other off from time to time. That was one of their war games.

Once he crossed the pipe, he would check the blackberry patch to see if they were ready. Then he would go along the path beside one of his favorite spots. There he saw all types of water life, crawfish, small snakes and little fish. Of course, it wouldn't have been complete without a frog. He had named him Teddy. Teddy knew what time his friend would appear every day. John always had a worm for him. John's time in the woods was so rewarding and relaxing, he enjoyed every moment. John and the other boys played all day. The day was coming to an end and John knew he had to go home. "Goodbye, my little friends," he said to the animals. "I'll see you tomorrow." He left the woods. Still thinking of the friend he had seen, John looked up the other path to see if the girl was there. Then he thought, *I hope I see her tomorrow. Yes, she will be here tomorrow.*

The next day, as the daylight started to break, it was clear that it had been raining really hard all night. It rained for a whole week until it finally stopped. This was their rainy season, and they were getting their share. It had never rained so much in this little town.

As the sun began to rise on the first clear day in over a week, John and Sarah arrived in the woods. She was coming down her path, and he was in his. Their eyes met for the first time. It was as if the rest of the world didn't exist. John felt as if he was being lifted up. He knew this was his special friend. Sara, meanwhile, felt a sense of royalty, as if she were a queen. She imagined the boy as a Black Knight, and they both were very happy to see each other. This time she saw him and was not frightened.

"Hello. How are you? I am John."

"I'm Sara."

"I didn't mean to frighten you the other day."

"Oh, it was nothing. I just didn't expect to see anyone else. This is my special place," Sara said.

"This my special place also," replied John.

As they looked at each other, electricity filled the air.

"What school do you attend?" Sara asked.

"I am at Carver. It is my last year and I really don't want to switch schools, but I have to next year."

"I attend Adcock."

"We will attend the same school next year," John said.

"That will be fun," replied Sara. Both were in the seventh grade, but would be in the eight next year.

"Have you lived here long?" asked John.

"We've lived here for a year, but I don't play with anyone."

"Would you like to play together?" asked John.

"Sure," replied Sara.

"Come on, I will show you all my hiding places." John introduced Sara to all his little creatures and showed her the bird's nest with eggs that were about to hatch. "They will have four beautiful little ones soon. Sara, it is so wonderful when the woods come to life. The trees grow so strong and with all the little families, we will have a wonderful time."

"I can't wait," said Sara.

The two played for weeks and became quite a team over the summer. They met everyday. Sara's father never knew, because he was still trying to save his job. Each day their hearts grew closer and closer, as two stars meeting in the night. John nicknamed her "Butterfly" because he thought she was the most beautiful creature in the world. She called him "Sunrise" because he used to love to see the sun come up. Everyday they played Mama and Papa, just like a happy family, not like the ones they were trying to escape.

John's friends didn't like the fact that he played with Sara everyday. They felt he had abandoned them. "Hi John," yelled Don. "Come and play with us, or will she let you?"

"Come on John," said Will, "we have a play house in a tree, but no girls are allowed."

"I can't," said John, "I am having fun with Sara."

Don responded by pushing Sara.

"Don't do that," warned John.

Don pushed Sara again. John grabbed him and they began to fight.

Sara asked the other boys to stop the fight, but they laughed. Soon she also jumped on Don, the other boys were shocked because they couldn't believe this. She could fight like a boy. John and Sara were really putting a beating on Don when the rest of the boys pulled them apart.

Will said, "Stop! Stop! Come on fellows, let's leave them alone. If he wants to play around with her, let him. Come on!"

Since Will was the leader of the group, all the boys started to leave with him. "That girl could fight like a boy," said one of the boys. "They were really putting a beating on you, Don. It's a good thing we pulled them off of you when we did."

John got up off the ground. "Are you okay?" he asked Sara.

"Yes, I am fine," she replied.

"I didn't know you could fight like that," said John.

"Well, there is only my brother and I, and he is younger than me. My dad showed me how to fight," replied Sara.

Don's friends couldn't stop laughing, but nevertheless they had to stop them from fighting. Everyone laughed as if they could not stop.

"Don, she had you, man," said Mike.

"Well, it was two against one," Don replied.

"Sara, you're all right," said Mike. "We like you, and you're welcome to hang with us anytime. Let's go fellows," and they all left. John and Sara never had any more problems again from his friends.

John and Sara had fun all summer. Life was so wonderful. They both enjoyed their friendship. Everyday it was as if it was meant to last forever. The woods soon came to life with all the little babies, and they looked in on all of them. One day, one of the little birds had fallen from its nest.

"Look, John, it's a little baby. He looks so frightened."

"Don't touch it, Sara. If you do, the mother will not feed it. I will go home and get some gloves. I read that it was safe."

"Okay, I will stay here and watch him."

"Look out for the mother because they can be mean," John said.

John ran home to get his gloves. As he returned, Sara yelled, "John, the mother bird is over there, it's a robin."

"Okay, watch her for me."

John got the baby bird and started up the tree. As he reached the nest the mother bird started toward him.

"John, look out, here she comes."

John ducked and the bird just missed him. Once he got down from the tree, she was making another dive.

"John, run, she is right behind you," Sara said. He ran out of the woods as fast as he could with the mother bird right behind him. Sara was behind them, also, laughing as hard as she could. That bird chased John all the way home.

While enjoying the woods, John and Sara built a house as though they were a family. Each day they made sure there were fresh fruits and vegetables. It was so peaceful in the woods, at the end of the day, they didn't want to leave. Yes, departing was bitter, but they both looked forward to the next day.

The next day always arrived quickly. Sara and John made their way to their special place. At the same time, they both began to speak. "Sara."

"John . . . I am sorry. You go first," said Sara.

"No, you go," replied John.

"Well, I have this feeling that we won't see each other again."

"That is strange," said John.

"What do you mean?"

"Because I was getting ready to tell you the same thing! I love you Sara, and I don't want to lose you. I lost one special friend, and I prayed for another and got you."

"I love you also, John, and I want to always be in your life."

"Why do we have this feeling?" asked John.

"I don't know, but my dad may lose his job any day and we may have to move."

"Yeah, but he is an engineer. He can find a job anywhere."

"Yes, but where? I think he wants to leave and if he goes, I won't go."

"Don't you worry, Sara. I will always love you and I won't let anybody take you from me."

At that point they began to kiss. It was sweet at first, but the deeper they looked at each other, the more they wanted to be one. John laid her down and she said, "Is this what we want to do?" Sara and John were afraid, but at that moment they wanted to share their whole life together. They didn't think of anything but being one forever. And this was their way of sharing that moment.

Wrong as it may have been, they were young and in love. They did not know what they felt, but at their age they had accepted each other as being married in their hearts. As they got dressed, stillness was in the air. They didn't realize what they had done. The feeling was strange, and it was their first time even thinking of each other that way. John finally broke the air.

"Listen, Sara, are you okay? We did not expect to do this. I feel bad, but I love you the same, if not more. Don't ever leave," said John.

"I won't. I promise," said Sara.

"Sara, we need to see if our parents will let us get married. We are both about thirteen years of age."

"No," said Sara, "my father would hit the roof. With the job giving him pressure, him and mom arguing everyday, if I tell him about you that would be the last straw. John I love you, but we are young and our parents would never let us do this."

"Sara, I understand, my cousin got married last year, but that was because she was pregnant. We don't need that yet," John replied.

"You're right, we don't need to do this again until we're married," Sara said.

"Sara, I will always love you, and when we are old enough I will ask for your hand, but you're my wife in my heart."

"I love you also, John, and will never love anyone but you for the rest of my life. In my heart you're my husband." As they kissed, neither had any idea it may be their last.

When the day had come to an end, they both went their separate ways. "I'll see you at school tomorrow, I love you Butterfly." As they left each other, they had no idea of how much their lives were going to change. They wanted to be together forever, but they didn't know how. They were only thirteen. Their parents would not even think of letting them get married at their age. How would they stay together forever?

Meanwhile, Sara's dad had just lost his job. He had already made plans to move to California. As Sara entered the house, her father said, "Get in here, young lady. Where have you been? You've been in those woods again. I told you to stay out of those woods. We won't have to worry about that anymore. Get packed, we are leaving."

"I don't want to go," Sara said. Mommy, do I have to?"

"Yes, you have to—we're a family. We have to stay together, honey, it will be okay," said Mrs. Moright.

"We have to be there tomorrow," her dad said.

"Be where?" asked Sara.

"You never mind, young lady, just get packed," replied her dad.

As they packed and left, John never knew. Sara didn't even get a change to even call him. The movers arrived and began packing the furniture and clothes. Their phone was already turned off. When they started for the airport, Sara saw her neighbor and knew she went to their school.

"Beverly! Please give this letter to John."

"Where are you going?" asked Beverly.

"I don't know—but I promise I will be back."

As Sara's family pulled out of the driveway, she had no idea if she would be back again. She wanted to return, but being young, your life and friends will change. All the way to the airport Sara could only think of John and how much she would miss him. She had no idea what was going to happen in their lives, but she hoped and prayed that they would always stay in love.

With her eyes filled with tears, she drifted off to sleep, for the ride to the airport was about two-and-a-half hours long. At last she was at rest and her mind was calm.

CHAPTER 4

Summer vacation was over and the next day school started. John looked everywhere for Sara. "Hi Bill. Have you seen Sara?" Bill was Beverly's older brother, who lived next door to Sara.

"Man, they left last night. Her father got a new job. Didn't she call you?"

"No. I guess she couldn't," John said.

"Here comes my sister, ask her," replied Bill.

Beverly was coming toward John. "Hi, John, I have something for you. Sara told me to make sure you got it." She reached into her book bag and gave him the letter.

"What is wrong? Where is she? Is everything okay?" asked John.

"Yes, everything is okay," replied Beverly. "She and her family had to move."

"Did she say where they were going, or anything?"

"No, but she said to make sure you got this letter." John took the letter and ran down the stairs and out of the building. He ran as fast as he could until he reached the woods. Once he reached the woods, he sat down on his favorite log. With tears in his eyes, John opened the letter slowly.

Dear John,

I love you. Dad got a new job and said we had to leave. I didn't even get a chance to call you. I'll miss you, but will never forget you; my love will never die. I will find you one day.

Love always,
Butterfly.

P.S., sometimes think of me. I'll always think of you. I don't know where his job is or where we are going. I will try to contact you. I love you, Sunshine.

As the letter fell to the ground, John was still crying. Sara's vision appeared for the first time ever. It was as if her image was real. John was afraid; he tried to move and could not.

The vision of Sara saw that he was afraid and began to speak. "Don't be afraid, John. It is I, Sara, and I am just a dream. They are silent dreams, but we will understand each other. I will be here when you need me."

"Sara, why did you have to go?"

"We're still young, John. My father made me go, he has to raise my brother and I. It will be all right, John. We will grow up one day and we will have control of our lives. Don't worry, I'll always love you." Her vision soon faded away.

John thought about Sara's smile. He would never forget, or stop loving her. His friend was gone; all that was left were her memories.

Sara's family arrived in California. The airport was so crowded; people were busy rushing everywhere. Sara was in her own little world. As they collected their bags, her mom tried to console her. "Sara, it's not so bad. I know you'll miss your friends, but you'll make new ones."

Sara's brother, William, was happy. "Mother can I take a picture?"

"Yes, dear."

"Can Sara be in it with me?"

"Yes, if she would like."

At first Sara didn't smile, then she thought of John. And the things he used to do to make her laugh. She was cheerful then, and posed for a pretty picture.

As they left the airport it began to sink in: they were in California to stay. The taxi drove up and down this beautiful city; the Moright's couldn't help but notice all the big buildings standing so tall. The people were everywhere, going back and forth, doing nothing it seemed. Everything was being done at a fast pace and they would have to adjust. As they pulled up to the door of their new home, the neighbors waved. There was a welcoming committee waiting in their new yard.

"Hi, Mr. and Mrs. Moright. I am Gina, and this is my husband Bill. Your brother let us know you were coming. He and his wife will be over later."

"My name is Jesse and this is my wife Betty."

"Come over here, children, meet our welcoming committee," Sara's mom said.

"Hello, Sara and William. You will love it here," said one of the new neighbor's kids. "We have good schools and all the kids are friendly. There are many places to play. We have lots of parks."

"Here is a gift for your family, Mrs. Moright. Please call me Betty."

"Well, Sara," said her dad. "What do you think, is this nice or what? Do you miss North Carolina?"

But Sara, still shocked by having to move, didn't answer. She just walked in the house to her room and sat on the bed. While there, a vision of John appeared to her for the first time. She saw him walking in the woods with his head down. He looked so sad, so lonely.

"John, John is it really you? I miss you so bad, but my father made me come."

"That's okay, Sara, I understand. We will always be in love and one day we will be together. We will grow up one day and then we can make our own decision. I love you and you remember that," and his vision faded as Sara's mom came into the room.

" Are you okay, baby?"

"Yes, Mother, I am fine."

"Who were you talking to?"

"Nobody, I was just talking out loud."

"Well, if you need to talk, let me know dear. I love you sweetheart."

"Yes, Mother, I will."

Two weeks later, as the family began to settle in the area, Sara woke up very ill. Her mother became very worried because she had an idea what it was... but she trusted Sara and didn't want to think of her having sex at her age.

"Sara!"

"Yes, Mom?"

"Have you been sexually active?"

Sara answered with an emphatic *no*.

"It's okay, you can tell me, I am your mother and I love you."

"No, Mother, I have not had sex with anyone."

Sara loved her parents and had never lied to them before. She was so afraid they would not like her anymore. She was also hoping she was not pregnant. This sickness had occurred several mornings since they had arrived. Sara thought she had managed to hide it. Her mother had seen it since day one.

"We have got to tell your father, Sara."

"Mom, he will be mad at me."

"Don't worry," said her mother, "he will figure it out sooner or later. It would be best to tell him. I will handle it tonight at dinner, I will tell him and hope he understands."

That evening when they had all sat down to dinner, Sara's mom said to her husband, "Honey, I need to talk to you after dinner."

"Okay," he replied. "Is everything okay?"

"Yes, but it's important that we have a talk concerning Sara." All eyes focused on Sara.

"Sara, are you still upset because we had to move? It is my responsibility to take care of my family and that I will. I love all of you but I have to do what is best for all of us. I wouldn't even think of leaving my little girl or boy behind. Sara, William, I need you both in my life. I love my family dearly. You'll just have to get over North Carolina and your friends."

As Sara began to speak in a defensive manner, her mother interrupted her before she could say much.

"Honey, let's talk after dinner."

Jesse continued, "We moved out here, and our kids will adjust."

Sara had placed her head down on the table the whole time her father was talking. Then once he finished she looked up.

"Mother, may I be excused from dinner? I am not hungry."

Her mother said, "Sure, Sara. Are you okay?"

"Yes, I'm just not hungry." As Sara went to her room, she heard her parent arguing.

William followed her to her room. "Are you okay sis? I wish I could help, but I am just a little boy."

"Yes, William, I know. I love you, my brother."

"I wish you would not say those things to her," said Mrs. Moright. "The child has feelings and you need to start recognizing them. You're driving her away. You're so busy being the Ruler of the House that you are forgetting how to be a father. Now, are you ready to listen to what I have to say?"

But Jesse stormed out of the house. "I'll be back."

"We need to talk. "

"Not now. I will talk to you later," he said as he got in his car and pulled out of the driveway.

Betty was thinking to herself, *How can my husband go to a bar and try to drown his problems away?* But she had to talk to him. *We can't run away from this problem, it's here to stay.*

Jesse returned home after two hours and went to bed. "Honey, is Sara okay?"

"No, I don't think so," Betty replied.

"Well, I am sorry I left out. I was just hoping the move would be good for us."

"Honey, it was good," said Mrs. Moright. "But it is something more."

"What do you mean?"

"She doesn't think you love her."

"Of course I do, she is my little girl."

"Well, brace yourself, your little girl may be pregnant."

"What! What did you say? How? There is no way this could be happening! Have you made plans to have her checked out by a doctor?"

"Yes, I have. Now calm down, dear. She will need us now more than ever, so get some sleep. There is nothing we can do about it tonight."

"I've been a good father. How could I let this happen?"

"It is not your fault," said Betty, "it's our fault, now go to sleep. We are a family and we will get through this together."

Soon the night was quiet, all was asleep.

Meanwhile in North Carolina, John was sick. His parents couldn't figure out the problem. When they took him to the hospital, the doctor couldn't find anything wrong with him.

"Doctor, he is mostly sick like a woman when she is

pregnant," said Mrs. Fields. "It's in the morning only."

"That is impossible," said the doctor. "Well, just give him these aspirins for a while and see if he runs a fever. We've done enough tests and he's fine."

John was afraid and asked his mom was he going to die.

"No, son, Momma will take good care of you," his mom said. Then they left the doctor's office.

As Sara arrived at the medical office the next morning, she was afraid. "Hello, Sara," said Doctor Bluebern. "How are you?"

"I have been waking up sick in the morning," said Sara.

"Have you ever had sex with anyone?" asked the doctor."

Sara immediately responded with a loud "NO."

"You can talk to me, Sara. I am your friend. We will run some tests on you, and they will tell us the truth."

"Well," said Sara, "I did have sex with this one boy before I left North Carolina. It was about three weeks ago. I got sick a week or two after that."

The doctor informed Sara's mother that he would call her next day, after the results of the test came in. The next day, the doctor called her.

"Mrs. Moright, this is Doctor Bluebern. Yes, the tests were positive. Your daughter is pregnant."

"Oh my God. How could this happen?"

"Your daughter said she had sex only once with a

young man her age before she left North Carolina. She was afraid to tell you because she didn't want you to be mad."

"Thank you, Doctor Bluebern."

As Sara arrived home, her mother told her the news. Now she had to tell her husband. When he arrived, she hoped he was in good mood.

As Jesse came home, Betty met him at the door. "We received the news from the doctor. She is pregnant!"

"How and by whom?"

"Well, she had sex only once with her friend from North Carolina, and she got pregnant."

"Well, we will have to deal with this."

"We can't think of an abortion," said Betty. "We are Christians."

"Where is Sara?"

"She's in her bedroom."

Jesse called out, "Sara, come in here."

As Sara entered the room, her parents saw the beautiful little girl who was about to become a mother before they wanted her to.

"Honey, you're pregnant. Now I am mad, but I love you. Just tell me how could you? Why did you?"

"It was an accident, Daddy."

"Accidents just don't happen, did you do this to punish me and your mother?"

"No, Daddy, I didn't. I am sorry," cried Sara.

"Well, you can bet your friend will never find out what happened. He must never know. Do you understand? We will help you, honey, you'll be okay. Sara, I love you. I am your father and I will always love you. I will be here for you. Give me a hug."

Sara listened to her father and she would never let John know. Sara felt more alone now than ever. She would come home from school and just stay in her room, her mom took great care of her. She soon started the home study, so she could continue school. The family did all they could to keep this from being hard on her. Even William pitched in and helped clean her room.

"I am going to be an uncle, Sis."

"Yes, you are, and you will be the best uncle in the world."

The embrace, love and joy that took place in this home is one that other families should practice and learn. Sure, Sara and John made a mistake. They used bad judgment at a very young age, but when something like this has happened it's too late to punish that child. We, as parents, need to be supportive before it happens, and if it does happen be very supportive after the fact. Let that child know that you'll be there for them. Let them also know that we all make mistakes. This is very important for their growth in life.

CHAPTER 5

As the months went by, Sara wondered about John. She sat in her room and wrote him letters everyday. She knew he may never see them, but if faith brought them together again she wanted to share all these things. She talked to her child often. Telling him about his dad, just as Jesus knew of God his Father. By the end of her pregnancy, she felt as if John was right there with them.

Meanwhile, John was feeling okay and going through his own little talks. He would go down to the woods and talk to Sara. He felt her presence with him. She would appear and talk to him every so often.

One morning while in the woods, her image appeared. She was pregnant.

"John, don't worry about me. I am pregnant with our child and we're fine. You won't see him until he is grown, but you'll see him, I promise. We are safe and thinking of you every day. He will know all about you. But I want to tell him your name. I am teaching him now, before he is born."

John reached out to Sara, but she was gone.

About that time, one of his friends walked up behind him.

"John?"

"Yes, Eddie."

"Are you okay, man?"

"Yes, I am fine."

"Whom were you talking to?"

"Oh, no one," replied John. "Just thinking out loud to myself."

"Man, don't let your parents hear you doing that," replied Eddie. "They'll think you're doing drugs."

"I know," said John, "they already think that. Especially my dad, he thinks I am weird. I am fine. Lets go play ball."

It was like a dream to him, and he could not understand it. She may be pregnant, what could he do then, and he began to get nervous. He ran out of the woods as fast as he could. When he got to the edge of the woods, he began to smile and think of how it would feel to have a child. His face was glowing with pride, but then he began to thing of his child growing up without him, and it made him sad. Then he began to cry. He knew that he had to find them, but he was too young to do anything. He thought, *One day I will find them, one day I will.*

Eddie saw the expression on John's face. He was worried about his friend and decided to keep a close eye on him. He knew John was sad because Sara had left him, so he spent as much time as he could with him.

The months passed by quickly and Sara went in the

hospital on her appointed date. Eight months, twenty-two days. She was in labor for about six hours. It was very painful, but her parents were with her the whole time. Her mom was in the room the whole time.

"Now, honey, I need you to breathe," said the doctor.

"Come on Sara, push. You are doing great. Honey," said her mom, "remember what we practiced. I will help you breathe. Come on, you can do this, come on." Sara soon started to breathe properly.

Back on the east coast, John was asleep because of the time change from coast to coast. All of a sudden, he sat up in his bed, climbed out on the chilly, wooden floor, and headed down the hallway toward the living room. His little brother woke up also and followed close behind him. John entered the living room and began to walk around and around in circles. He was breathing hard and murmuring about something. His brother ran to their parents' bedroom.

"Mom, Dad, Mom, Dad, come quickly, John has lost his mind."

As Larry and Rebecca got up, Larry asked groggily, "Now what is it, a fire? Is the house on fire?"

Rebecca was the first to get to John. As she entered the room, she saw him walking and asked, "John what's wrong?" Then she could see he was asleep.

"Breath, breath, relax, relax. Come on, count, you can do it. Don't stop," yelled John, "you're doing fine."

By this time everyone was awake in the house. John sisters and brothers thought he was possessed. "Mom, what is wrong with him?" asked Mona.

Larry finally entered the room. "What the hell?"

"Shush, honey," said Rebecca. "He's sleepwalking."

"He is doing what?" asked Larry. "I've only seen that on TV—are you sure he's not on drugs?"

"Now, dear, you know he's not on drugs," said Rebecca, "and when someone is sleepwalking, we're not suppose to wake them."

"Breathe, push, breathe, push, you can do it. I see him, I see him."

"You sure this boy is not on drugs ? See who?" asked-said Larry. "What is this kid dreaming about?"

"Maybe he saw a movie about someone having a baby, or maybe he's psychic and can see someone having a baby for real," said Rebecca.

"He is just plain crazy," said Mona.

Then all of a sudden John stopped. "It's a boy! Yes, a boy." Then he turned and went down the hallway into his room, with everyone behind him, and lay down, asleep and still once again.

"This is totally wild, isn't it?" said Mona?

"All right, all right, everyone back to bed." The house was quiet once again.

"Honey," said Larry, "I want you to get that boy tested for drugs."

"Nonsense," said Rebecca, "you know he is not on drugs. He was just sleepwalking, now go back to sleep."

Back in California, Sara was delivering her baby at the same time this was happening. "I see the head. Come on, push!" the doctor yelled.

"Come on, Sara," said her mom. "You can do it." As Sara pushed and screamed, a boy, John Jessie Hart, was born at five minutes after twelve AM, August twenty-eighth. He was five pounds and four ounces. The little fellow looked as if he changed color three times.

"He is beautiful," said Sara's mother.

"Here is your son," and the nurse handed Sara her baby.

"He looks just like his daddy," Sara said.

"He looks just like you," beamed her mom. "What do you want to name him?"

"Name him John Jessie Moright."

"My first grandchild," said her mother."

But Sara, thinking of John, could only cry and wish that he were there.

"Sara, you and your child will be fine," said the doctor as he left the room.

Sara's father and brother came into the room, just as the doctor was leaving. Her mom held the baby.

"He is so handsome," she said. Then she showed him to his uncle. "This is your nephew," she told William. William was eight years old. As he looked at his nephew, he touched the baby's face.

"He is handsome, Mommy."

"Yes he is, son. Now let's go so she can get some rest."

Sara took her son back and with a smile said, "Your dad is going to be so proud of you. I will call you LJ, short for Little John."

"But his last name will be Hart, which is your mother's

maiden name," said her dad. "If we name him Moright, then your friend may know. We will help you raise him and you can see him once you're old enough."

True to his word, Mr. Moright and his wife were there to help Sara. They had her room ready when she came home from the hospital. William had drawn some nice pictures for her and Little John. They were on the walls. As the months went by, they all worked hard to see that Sara was happy and getting the care she needed. LJ was family and everyone loved him so much.

Sara and her son began enjoying life. She talked to him about his dad every day. Although she told him of his father, she would never mention his real name. That he would never know about until faith stepped in.

Time passed by quickly the first year, and all the family pulled together to help. Sara's father loved the child so much. It changed his life and he was a different person.

One year later Little John was just beginning to walk. Sara said, "Look mother. He is trying to walk. Come on, come on. He's going to fall."

"No Sara," said her mother. "Let him go. I let you walk the same way." He took two steps and sat down. It was so sweet and gentle to see him going down in slow motion.

He sat down soft and as he did he said his first word: "Daddy."

"Did you hear that, Mom?"

"Yes I did," said Sara's mother. "I have heard kids that age say half a word before, but not a whole one," she said.

"He is a special child, Mom," said Sara, "and I love him very much. I talk to him about his dad every day. One day he will see him."

Sara started back to school and was very active in her work. She and a couple of girls who were also mothers, along with two teachers, formed a club called "ICHTY." It stood for "It Could Happen To You." It was supposed to teach young people about the responsibility of having kids at a very young age. Each member would talk about their life before and after their child was born. It also was set up for the parents of the young mothers to attend. The older adults in the group would talk about dealing with your child, and grandchild, after the fact.

Sara was the youngest lady in her school to have a child. She was also the hardest worker in the group. The group held meetings every week, and traveled to other schools to hold seminars.

Pretty soon ICHTY had gone national and was recognized by the state of California as one of the leading non-profit organizations every formed. Wilmot High School in California, the school Sara attended, received the State Education Award. Sara and the ladies who formed the group were presented the award at a special ceremony.

Other schools joined in, and within a year there were over five hundred schools nation wide as part of this group. Yes, it must be mentioned also that there were just as many male members as there were females.

Yes, time was flying it seem for Sara and her son. I will tell you about a special night in young LJ's life.

Sara had tucked her son in to bed after a busy day. She said, "LJ, don't forget to pray for Daddy." His little eyes were filled with love for a man he had never seen. "Now you lay down," she said, and gave him a big kiss. "I love you, my son," she said with all her heart. She began their prayer, "Lord, lay me down to sleep..." and soon they both were at rest.

Later that night while the house was as quiet as it gets, LJ woke up and climbed out of bed. Even though it was dark, he didn't let that stop his curiosity as a child. He headed down the hallway as he left his mom's room. Sara was still asleep, and so was everyone in the house. He looked in everyone's bedroom to make sure. Like all kids do, LJ headed for the kitchen. Once there, he opened the fridge and found his favorite food. Yes, you guessed it—cheese. All kids love cheese, it seems, and now he had his.

He grabbed several slices and went to a hiding place he had seen before. One day his grandfather was working on the sinks in the kitchen and he was helping. "Papa," he had said, "I like this spot."

"Yes," replied his grandfather. "I like it also. We can hide in here when your mother and grandmother are looking for us."

There LJ was, safe and sound in this special place.

Sara was awakened by that motherly instinct and looked around for LJ. But he was nowhere to be found. "LJ, LJ!" she called in a very low voice, trying not to wake the house. No answer was heard, so she got up to look for her son.

Her first stop was her mom's room. She knocked on the door. "Yes?" called her mom.

Sara opened the door and walked in. "Mom, I can't find LJ."

Her mom sat up and in a nervous voice said, "What do you mean you can't find him?"

"Well, we went to bed, he was at my side, and now he is gone."

"Did you check William's room?"

"No," replied Sara, "this is my first stop."

Sara and her mother set out to find him. "I will check William's room, Mom."

"Okay, I will check the bathroom," said Mrs. Moright.

He was not in William's room. He was not in the bathroom, either, and they both started to get worried.

"Before we wake your father, let's go downstairs," said Mrs. Moright.

As they headed downstairs, both women were trying not to imagine anything bad. Sara, being the mother, had a very worried look.

"Don't worry," said her mom. "He can't get out of the house, all doors and windows are locked."

Once downstairs they split up to look for him.

"I will look in the living room and down the hall," said her mom.

"Okay, I will check the kitchen, because kids love to go in the fridge," replied Sara. As she went in the kitchen her eyes were like search lights in the sky. "LJ, LJ!" she called out. But there was no answer.

LJ heard his mom but he was afraid to answer her because he thought he would get in trouble. Sara turned to leave the room when she heard a bumping noise, which sounded like it came from the cabinet.

She went to look. As she opened the cabinet under the sink, there was her son. Sitting there so pretty, like a squirrel on limb. "My baby!" she cried out. "You had me so worried! My baby!"

About that time her mother walked in. "Here he is, Mom, safe and sound." Mrs. Moright and Sara laughed because there was LJ, sitting in the dark, eating cheese like he didn't have a care in the world.

"Mom," said Sara, "this is so pretty."

"Yes it is," replied her mom, "wait, I will get the camera." They snapped the photo as LJ looked on with surprise.

"Come to me, my son," called Sara. LJ climbed out from under the sink, which had kept him so safe. They all went back to bed and the night was quiet once again.

CHAPTER 6

The years passed quickly, and Sara did fine with LJ. He was so smart that he started pre-school early, and did well there. Sara was voted president of her class. She was the first-ever female to hold that post. While in school, she kept her head in the books, and raised LJ right.

"Mom?"

"Yes, Sara?"

"I've been offered a scholarship to study biology next year."

"That is wonderful, but is it what you want?"

"Yes, I love studying about life in the world."

"Well, whatever you choose will be fine with your dad and I. Besides, it is only ten minutes away. You can live here and drive to school."

Yes, things were working out for Sara after all. But she still wondered what John was doing. Even though she could see him in her dreams, did she see what his life really was, or was it something she was imagining?

Both John and Sara were doing well in life, but still they were in love and missed each other. They both had an idea of what the other was thinking by the dreams they were having, but they were not sure. Each worked hard in school and for their community. Yes, their lives were coming together sooner than they would have imagined, but to them it seemed like a long time.

Their son, LJ, was five years old and in kindergarten. He was as smart as his parents. He loved the woods. His mother took him to the park and to the woods every chance she could. He asked his mom about his dad every day. She shared all of their moments with him. He would just sit and listen until he fell asleep.

Sara told LJ that his dad was a good tree climber. He loved the woods, it was where he always went to think and write. She went on to tell him that they both would go to the woods before the sun came out, so they could see it rise over the trees. Sara told LJ that her nickname was Butterfly, and his father's was Sunshine. She told LJ that all the animals loved his father, and he could make them come right to him.

She went on to say, "I remember one time this little bird had fallen from his nest and your dad wanted to put him back. He always read books so he knew not to touch them with his hands, so he ran home to get some gloves. Once he got back he placed the baby bird in its nest. I was looking out for the mother, and there she was. "John," I yelled, "there she is and she is coming for you. Hurry, hurry and get down." Once he climbed down, the mother bird chased him all the way home. It was so funny. I miss him a lot," she said. "And I feel he misses me, too. One day we will see him. One day we will."

"Mom, what is my dad's name?" asked LJ.

"His name is Kenneth Jones," she hesitantly lied, "but he is far away."

"You will see him one day, I promise, but the time is not right now. I promised my father I wouldn't try and find your father until I was grown." LJ would just sit, wonder, and listen until he fell asleep.

Obeying her father's wishes, Sara never tried to find John, and he never tried to find her. They were young and didn't know how to contact one another. Besides that, faith was in control of them and it was not time for them to be together at their young age.

The years continued to pass quickly and they were growing up. John and Sara were getting ready to graduate from high school. They both had excelled in academics and in sports.

Sara had played basketball her senior year. That was the only year she played organized sports, and turned out to be one of the top guards in the league. She averaged twelve points and six steals a game. She was offered a scholarship to play in college, but chose to be a scientist instead. She received a full scholarship in biology and attended a school near her home. Her parents were pleased with her decision and would still be there for her while she went through college.

Meanwhile, John Fields set all of North Carolina state's

records in football as a wide receiver. He was also one of the top four hundred-meter guys around. His grade point average was very good, staying at three point five for three years. He chose to stay near home also.

He graduated with honors from high school, then accepted a scholarship to attend Livingston University—a small black college in North Carolina—to play football and run track. He was the top player in the state and could have gone to any school he wanted, so people wondered why he chose to stay so close to home. He felt it was the person who made the difference, and not so much the school. Livingston is one of the oldest black colleges around and has a lot of history. This John liked, and he knew he would make the school proud of him.

The campus was so beautiful that it looked as if God had just placed it there for John and the other students that went there. John and his parents knew he would get a good education there.

First Baptist, the church that John attended, did something special every year for the kids at high school graduation. Before they all went to college or the military the church would give them a certificate of appreciation for being so faithful and wishing them well in life. This helped all the kids to do well in whatever they did.

It was Sunday, May twenty-first, and everyone looked beautiful. The choir wore their best robes for this event. John sang in the young adult choir. Each choir had to sing three selections. The youth choir started the program off with a song that only a child could sing, and it was beautiful. Everyone in the church said that song was made for Marcus, the kid who sang the solo.

Once they finished, the young adult choir was next. On this day they sang so great it was like a sermon sent from GOD. The choir came in through the front door. The ushers opened up, and they walked in dancing and clapping their hands. Soon everyone joined in and with no words at all everyone was on their feet. The director raised her hands and they stopped. Then they sang their first song and it was beautiful.

Once they finished, the adults came in through the side doors. Usually they sang songs to remind them of the past and keep the old gospel alive, but today they had a surprise for the kids. They had listened to some music by singers of younger ages to let the kids of the church know how much they love them. They sang the new songs and did a wonderful job. They came in singing, and went out doing the same, with the congregation wishing for more.

One of John's friends, Emanuel, said "Man, would you listen to that. They can sing anything!"

As they finished their last song the minister started to speak. "Let's give them all a big hand. Every choir sounded so wonderful, and as the adult choir sang, yes all things are possible."

The minister preached that day. John didn't know that one man could take a verse from a song and preach so long. He found out that man is not doing it, God speaks through them, and when the minister finished there was joy in our church. The deacons took over after he finished.

"Now we come to that point in our program where we recognize the young adults who are graduating from high school," one of the deacons said. "We have kids going to college, the military and to regular jobs." They called out twelve names and yes, John Fields was among them. Every kid received a gift and some money to help him or her on their journey. They all received a Bible to let them continue to study the word and keep faith.

Afterward, the twelve graduates sang the church song. It was a very special day and everyone had a great time praying to GOD. The last thing the minister said to them was "May the LORD always teach and guide you in the direction He wants you to go. Amen."

During spring football practice, John Fields was the one everybody came to see. For the first time in years the media showed up to film some of their practices. All the alumni were excited because they had losing seasons for ten years, and now things may change.

At the start of he season, the word was out; John was already considered one the best wide receivers in the league and hadn't played a game. During his first year at Livingston he set a lot of records. In the opening game, against Florida Duburk University, he caught a touchdown pass and rushed for another one on an 80-yard run. After the game his coach gave him the game ball for offense.

"John," yelled the coach, "front and center. This young

man came to our program to help us win. He said, 'Coach, if I can't help, I don't want to be here.' Well, let me welcome you, Mr. Fields," and the coach shook John's hand as the team clapped on.

Every game was special to John because he played near home and his family could see him play. His freshman year was a record-setting year, but he could never get Sara off his mind. He found a special place on campus, and she would appear and they would talk. Still, their time to be together was not yet.

Going into his sophomore year in football, John had a better year than his first. The pressure was off from the media and the league. Everyone knew this young man could play. He may be at a small black college, but he was on the entire pro coaches list. The stadiums were full every game, and Livingston was winning once again. Over the next three years they would do just that—win.

As John Fields excelled on the field, he also excelled in the classroom. He was junior class president, and at the top of his class as far as grade point average. He also had projects in his community he helped start. He still did all he could for the elderly and kids. They had started a fun run that raised ten thousand dollars for the year, and another ten thousand which they used to purchase land to build a community center one day. Yes, their plans seemed to be coming into place. John was living up to his dreams. By working hard in everything he did, things were falling into place for him and the lady he loved so much.

As he finished his senior year in football, no one ever

thought he would make it. Not because of his books or lack of trying, but because he was that good. This young man could have gone pro straight from high school, but he promised his mom that he would get his education—and he did. Everything was special in John's life.

It must be mentioned that he had met a young lady at the beginning of his senior year. They became very close friends, but remembering Sara, he would never let their relationship go beyond that. He took her to the movies and the park quite often, and they shared a lot of great time together, but the intensity of his dreams was getting strong. He could never get his first love out of his mind. Not saying he wanted to get Sara out of his mind, because they felt each other's love all the time.

Often in the woods, the vision of Sara would tell John things he couldn't understand. This really did seem like a dream to him. It frightened both of them very much but whom could they talk to?

He still wouldn't let that stop him from relaxing and doing things he loved. He would go to the woods every chance he could. Sara's vision would come to him every so often. One day she appeared to him to let him know he had a son. As he sat in the woods on his favorite log, her vision appeared.

"John, John," she said so softly and sweet. He was heavy in thought and didn't hear her at first.

"Yes Sara, yes. I miss you, Butterfly."

"I miss you also, my Sunshine. Our time will be soon, but to you and me it will seem long, John," said Sara, "but don't worry, we will be together soon. I have a son, John."

"What?" said John. "You have a child?"

"Yes, your child. He is as smart and wonderful as you are. John, your son is growing up strong. I know you don't know him or even that he exists, but he will need you soon, so be strong and never stop believing in me or him. I miss you and our faith is getting closer every day."

"Sara, Sara...," then it faded. John was worried so much by his dreams, he decided to tell his friend, Sandra, about what was happening in his life.

One night while coming from the movies, he started to tell her what was on his mind. "Sandra, I like you a lot, but I don't think I can fall in love with another woman until I find Sara."

"Who is Sara, you mentioned her before?" Sandra kept talking. "This is the reason...?" and John's mind wander to the future and Sara.

"Sara, why do we have to be apart anymore? I need you." But she didn't answer and John couldn't understand.

"John, do not worry, we will be together, stay strong for your son. He will need you soon. He will need you."

John began screaming in his mind, *Sara I will find you, I will.* Soon her vision started to fade. *I love you, Sara, and I will always be here for you.* After that dream he knew she was still in his life.

John knew he would see them one day. "John, John," yelled Sandra. "Are you listening to me?"

"Yes, I am, but my dreams are so strong that they seem real and I feel like I am living two lives. I feel like I am going crazy."

"I like you John, but you have had this wall built up. Is Sara the reason why?"

"Well, yes, she comes to me in my dreams, or when I am in the woods thinking. It is as if she is there for real."

"John, you are scaring me."

"I am sorry," he replied. "I don't mean to, but you need to know so you won't think I am weird or something."

"You're doing a lot of things in life," replied Sandra, "and I just figured you had a lot on your mind."

"Well, one day I was in the woods and her vision came to me. She was just there—you're not going to believe this, I know. I could almost touch her. She was pregnant with a child and said it was mine. It was so real that I couldn't believe it. I was afraid and tried to run. My feet wouldn't move. When she finish talking, I ran out of the woods as fast as I could."

"That is so sweet," said Sandra.

"Her father moved her away when we were twelve years old."

"John, you could be thinking all these things because you miss her."

"Yeah, you're right. But what if it is true? That I do have a child out there somewhere."

"John, you were only twelve years old, I doubt it. She was too young to bear a child, and it was the first and only time, wasn't it?"

"Yes, I still can't help but wonder if she is okay. Our

faith is what keeps us together. We vowed to never stop loving each other, and I can't break that promise until I have seen her, to know if we still love each other."

Before Sandra could answer, four guys stopped them. Three of them grabbed John, and the other put a knife at Sandra's throat.

"Don't move or I'll cut her throat. So you are the star of the football team."

"Don't hurt her," yelled John. "What do you want?"

"We want you, Super Star. We lost a lot of money against you over the years. Yeah, and we won't lose any more," said one of the boys. Then they started to beat him with baseball bats.

"Stop," screamed Sandra. "Stop or you'll kill him."

Ignoring Sandra, the boys continued to beat John until finally the leader told them that it was enough. He then knocked her down next to John.

"He won't run again," one of the boys yelled, as they all ran away.

Sandra was screaming for help as John lay in a pool of blood. Several people passing by ran over to the couple and called the ambulance that rushed him to University hospital. At the hospital, they had to rush him into the operating room as the nurse called his parents. The detective who was called to handle the case took over, and spoke to Mr. Fields.

"Mr. Fields, this is Detective Givens. There has been an accident. Your son is hurt and we need you to come to the hospital immediately."

"What happened?" asked Mr. Fields.

"Mr. Fields, I can't talk over the phone, but please drive safely and get here. We need you here now."

John's parents made it to the hospital as fast as they could, only to find that their son had slipped into a coma. When they talked to Doctor Mills, he said that they had to operate or John may die. John's parents told the doctor to do whatever he had to do to save their son. Mrs. Field sat down and began to pray.

While in a coma, John started to dream. He was walking down a long, dark street. There was a dim light at the very end. The closer and closer he got to the light, he could see there were two people standing, waiting on someone, a lady and little boy.

"John," the lady cried out, "you have to wake up John, your son needs you. John this is your son. His name is John also. He will need you soon."

"Daddy, Daddy. I want to meet you. I want to get to know you, please wake up and be strong for us."

"Please wake up, John," cried Sara.

John responded as they began to fade. "Sara, please don't go."

"You must wake up and get strong for your son, because when the time is right, you will know him."

"Sara, Sara."

"Now wake up, you must wake up..." and the dream was over.

The doctor entered the room. "Mr. and Mrs. Fields, the operation was a success. The rest is up to him."

"May we see him?"

"Yes, but he's still in a coma."

Mr. And Mrs. Fields entered the room where their son lay in a lifeless state. With tears in their eyes, and a feeling of nothing but sadness, they could only wonder why, why their son?

As they each stood on the right side of his bed, Mrs. Fields grasped her son's hand and held it tight. "John, can you hear me?" She said in a quiet tone. The doctor told them that John may be in this state for a while, or he could just wake up. Mrs. Fields said "I don't care how long it takes, I am not leaving the hospital until you wake up, son. I will be here every minute. I know you will wake up."

Mrs. Fields stayed, and day after day she prayed for her son. One week later, John finally came out of his coma. When he opened his eyes, he looked around the room, not knowing where he was at first or what had happened. He began to smile and thanked GOD as he saw his mother sitting in a chair beside the window. She had never left his side.

"Momma."

As she woke up and saw his smile, she rushed to the bed with tears of joy in her eyes. "I knew you would come back to me son. I knew God would take care of you. Thank you, Lord," said Mrs. Fields in a very joyful voice.

"Momma. I am hungry," cried John.

"Now that's my son, you'll be fine."

"How long have I been here?"

"Eight days," replied Mrs. Fields. "The doctor said that you would be okay."

"Is Sandra okay?"

"Yes, she is fine. The police caught the young men who did this, they're from another college."

"Why me momma? Why?"

"I don't know," his mother replied, "but you get your rest now and we will talk later, your dad and I will be back."

Meanwhile, in California, Sara felt the pain that John was going through, but didn't know how to explain it to LJ. "Mom, what's wrong?" LJ asked.

"Nothing, son, I am sorry I got lost in my thoughts. I just wish you could see your dad. I miss him and I feel he misses me also. I hope we will see him soon."

Sara, although not with John, shared every pain he felt, and he hers. Their love for each other was real, but they were not meant to be together yet. Sara went into her room to relax, and John's image appeared.

"Sara, Sara."

As she looked up with tears in her eyes, she replied, "Yes, John?"

"I am fine and we will be together one day soon. Take care of LJ; I'll always love you." Then his vision faded. Sara laid down on the bed and went to sleep. Her mind was at peace now, and she didn't worry about him any more.

CHAPTER 7

Sara never met anyone she wanted to be serious with after John. Just like John, her visions and love were too strong. She knew she was in love with him and that she only cared for their son. She buried her feelings in hard work and LJ. Sure, she dated and lived a normal life, but her heart was set. She had some nice friends in her life, but no one could replace John Fields, and she wouldn't let a friendship go past that. Where was all this energy and love coming from for her and John? Its simple, we call it faith and it lives in all of us. She graduated from college with honors and became a scientist at a lab in California near her home.

LJ was in the sixth grade, was and excelling faster than most students. He always wondered about his dad. What does he look like? How old is he and how big is he? Does he play sports or what does he do? There was a lot going through his little head about the man his mother was so in love with.

She had told him all about their past, but *how is my dad now?* he wondered with excitement. *What is he doing? Is he thinking of us at all? Or does he even know of me?*

LJ's little eyes were always filled with tears when he spoke of this man. He was thinking of trying to find him one day, even as a little boy, but one night in a dream he was shown the future and told not to find his dad. So he relaxed and stopped worrying his mom so much. LJ, like his dad, was filled with wisdom from his granddad even as a young man, so he began to understand things going on in his life.

One month later LJ played defensive back on the youth football team. His mother and grandparents watched him play all the time. Sara's dad loved her son so much and treated him so well. It was like a new chapter in his life. Since LJ's birth, Sara's father had taken on a different role in life. He seemed like a changed man, not that he was bad or anything, but he seemed more of a father. Sara thought her father's job, and her son, was good for him. Maybe the move was not bad after all. Her parents were closer than ever now. Yet, when she was alone, she could only think of the one she had left behind: her one true love, John Fields. Still, her father had changed and that was good for her mom.

Her father, William, and LJ were very close and did so much together. To William LJ was like the brother he never had. They played together all the time and really grew up as the best of friends.

LJ loved sports, just like his dad. In the sixth grade still, he was bigger than the other kids. They couldn't let him run the ball as a running back, he was over the weight limit by one pound. To kids, one pound was like ten pounds on an adult. It was very hard to lose. The league had a weight limit on certain positions, and running back was one of them. The coach had to make a decision and made him a defensive back. Their team was called the Eagles, and they were always one of the best teams in the league.

LJ was the best runner on their team and coach Jones didn't think it was right to hold him back because he was a pound overweight. All year long, if any player on any team was over weight, they could not play in that position. Whichever team was leading by thirty points, had to take out their top players so their team couldn't continue to score and embarrass the other kids.

Coach Jones was a good coach and didn't wish to play those that were not fully developed for the game at there age. It was dangerous, and the kids mind might be affected by the trauma of being hit by bigger kids. That was why he fought the rules. He knew his players well enough, and didn't want to put a kid in a position to get hurt. They were a good football team, with some of the best players around. They won every game in their regular season and got a chance to play the championships in the next city.

As the game began, it was nice and sunny on this particular day. The Eagles were set to kick the ball off to the Beavers of Concord. Coach Jones told his kicker to place it as deep as he could in the end zone.

The Beavers started to move the ball on their own

twenty yard line. On the first series of plays, quarterback Bill Sanders drove the ball down the field for a score. The extra point was missed, and the Beavers led the game six to nothing.

The Beavers kicked off, and the Eagles brought it out to the forty yard line to start their drive. On the first play they were pushed back on a motion penalty. At second and fifteen on their twenty-five yard line, they started to move the ball on drives up the middle. The Eagles, like the Beavers, drove the ball down the field and scored. The extra point was missed, and the score was tied at six by the end of the first quarter. It must be noted that these kids were young, and some were small for their ages. To kids, extra points at this level are not expected, but the coaches have to start training young kickers early. That's why they let the kids try this. The kids loved it also. Every once in awhile a kid would kick one through the uprights and the whole stadium would go crazy.

The second quarter was scoreless, with both team's defenses showing a lot of heart. LJ had knocked down two passes, and made four individual tackles, to keep them out of the end zone in the first half.

Half time finally arrived, and both teams needed to regroup for the second half. In the Eagles's locker room it was quiet. Coach Jones walked in and started to speak.

"Listen, guys, we have got to play harder. We have given them six points. Tray, how many times did I tell you to never leave the middle?" asked the coach.

Tray is the middle linebacker for the Eagles.

"We know they are running away from LJ," said Coach Jones. "We need to use that to our advantage. Now, when we go out, we need to get the ball to LJ, and this is what I want you to do."

Both teams returned to the field for the second half of the game, which was going to be one of the best games this league had seen in years. The Eagles received the ball, and LJ brought it out of the end zone. Once he passed the twenty yard line he cut left, and was heading for a score but the other team's defense met him on the fifty yard line and saved a score.

Neither team could get any momentum going. At the end of the third quarter the game was still tied at six.

The Beavers had the ball at the start of the forth quarter. They put a good drive together, only to come up thirty yards short of the end zone. They turned the ball over to the Eagles on downs, and now it was their turn with only five minutes remaining in a well-coached, well-played game.

On the first play the Eagles ran right up the middle on a fullback dive, which netted them three yards and a second down. Second down, and seven yards to go, the coach called a pass to the tight end. The pass was knocked down, but if the tight end had caught the ball he would have had clear sailing to the end zone.

At third down and seven on the thirty yard line of the Beavers, the Eagles needed a great play because time was running out. Only thirty seconds remained in the game and the Eagles called a time out.

"LJ!" yelled the coach.

"Yes, Coach?" replied LJ.

"Remember the play we talked over in the locker room?"

"Yes, Coach," he replied.

"Well, it is time to run it. Everyone has to block well in order for this to work, okay?" yelled the coach.

"Okay," the team yelled back.

The quarterback called the signals, and LJ went in to motion to the right. Once the ball was in the quarterback's hands, he started to the left—toward LJ, who was running a reverse. They couldn't hand the ball off to him, so the coach told the quarterback to get hit and fumble the ball. It was not legal, but if it looked real no one would ever know.

"It worked, it worked!" yelled an assistant coach.

Both teams began yelling "Fumble, fumble, get the ball!"

You know who picked up the ball, yes, LJ. Now the kids on the other team were as big as he was. He began to run around to the left once he got the ball. Two guys hit him in the backfield, but he broke through and began down the field. Before he crossed the line, two more hit him. He ran he past those two, and another hit him. Every player on the other team hit him it seemed, but he would not stop. That boy was determined to score. Time was running out, but it didn't matter because LJ was headed for a score.

Finally, he was clear of all the players on the team,

running free like a pegasus in flight. He was twenty yards to the end zone and time had expired. Ten yards from the end zone, and to a score in one of the best games these young men had ever played. All of a sudden one of the craziest things happened. LJ began to tumble. He tumbled, and tumbled, and tumbled until he hit the ground.

Everyone was standing and cheering for LJ, and there he was going down, as time seemed to stand still. Once he cleared all the other players, he tripped himself and began to fall to earth like a bird that has lost flight. As he fell to earth, LJ thought to himself, *I don't believe this is happening, I fell five yards from a score. All that work and all that sweat, just to trip and fall.*

His coach ran out on the field, with the teammates following him. The coach hugged LJ as they all began to cry.

"I had it, Coach, I had it."

His little face was so sad and full of tears. People in the stands were crying also. It was one of the most touching moments you would have ever seen. The other team hugged LJ also. They felt his pain. LJ would never forget it. He still loved the game and said he would be good one day.

Sara, now out of college and working full-time, went to look for a house for herself and LJ. She wanted to live close to her parents.

"I don't know why you have to move," said her dad. "We have plenty of rooms."

"I know, but you and Mom have done enough. It's time for you to let go. William is getting ready to graduate and go to college. You can enjoy life a little. Dad, I love you and we won't be far. You can still see your grandson anytime you wish."

Sara was thinking about going to North Carolina to try and find John, now that she could. *Maybe he won't know me, or maybe he'll be in love with someone else,* she thought. It was a chance she was willing to take.

John, on the other hand, was thinking of going to school in California, but he was afraid of what he might find. *She has probably forgotten me. My dreams may not be real.* He thought he was crazy at times, or just in love with a dream.

One day while John was in church, the minister made a statement that seemed directed at him. It was a message from God he thought.

"Do not try and build your own faith, trust in God and let him give it to you."

When John left that service, he knew what it meant and decided against going to California.

Although he and Sara still had the silent dreams, their dreams had changed. Instead of missing one another, they were more about faith.

Sara would tell John that faith would bring them together soon, and not to worry. LJ, still wishing to meet him, began to understand also. He began to see things while he slept, and feel things as he grew in life.

John Fields now a senior at the University of Livingston, and currently running track. Their team was at a meet at North Carolina State University, The ACC Relays.

"John, where are you planning on playing football?" one of his teammates asked.

"Well, the Dallas Cowboys are my favorite," John replied. "I hope they draft me next month."

"I think you will get your wish," his teammate replied. You are a pretty lucky guy. How many people live through a coma and come back to be one of the best quarter-milers in the state in just three months?"

"Yeah," said John, "but the draft is for the weak teams first, and we know who that is."

At this time, Coach Bowall said, "John, it is time for the mile relay. Get the guys ready." So John and the other three guys started to get ready.

"Man, we need to win this to make the National," said Jody, one of the members of the team. The other two members were Shane Lawson and Will Bentley. John ran the last leg.

"Now keep us close," John yelled at Jody, who was to start the relay. The coaches circled around the judge and drew for lanes. John was focused more than he had ever been before. He always got into his own little world before he ran an event. As he went to find a quiet place to focus for a few minutes, the rest of the team got ready.

As I stand here, John prayed, *Lord, let us run a good and clean race.* All of a sudden his mind was in the sky as if he was flying. He was going in and out of clouds. His mind was relaxing. The heavens were so blue and beautiful. *Lord, this is so nice. I feel like a bird in flight.*

"John, John," yelled his coach. "Let's go."

His teammates would leave him alone. It was if he was a different person.

The teams all gathered on the track. John's team had drawn the first lane, the one his teammates didn't like. It didn't matter to John, he loved them all.

The first lap was ready to begin. "Come on, Jody, you have to make up your staggers in order to be in position when you come out of the final turn," yelled the coach.

The runners were set, the gun sounded, and Jody was off. He was running strong. "Run Jody, run," his team yelled. Half way around the turn, Jody was looking good, running smooth, and picked it up more. When they came out of the last turn, he was ahead. "Come on come on," yelled his teammates. As he reached the start/finish line, he was in first place.

The next in line was Shane. He took the baton and was off and running. "Go, Shane, go." yelled John. "Yea, Yea."

The runners for the next lap were in place, waiting for their hand-offs. Shane ran hard and smooth the whole backstretch. "Look at Shane run," yelled the coach.

When Shane went into the turn, the other runners started to gain on him. He was about ten yards ahead. The second and third team behind caught up to him on the outside. Shane came down the straightaway in third place, and handed the baton off to Will. He went into the first curve two or three yards ahead of one of the other teams, but was seven yards behind the two runners in front when he came out of the curve. As he pressed harder, everyone could see he had gained about five yards on the two teams out front.

There he went, running strong down the backstretch, and all the teams were close. He ran to the line where John was waiting.

"Come on, run hard. Don't stop," yelled John. John then took off and William ran through, handing him the baton. The race was on—this was it. The best runners are on the first and last legs. John was one of the best. He ran differently than anyone in the race. An opponent might catch him on the first two hundred yards, but his strong point was the last yards of the race. All three teams were about even at the half way mark.

John started to make his move in the curve; he would imagine a gun going off in his head. Then he really started to run. This is something he picked up in high school. The guys he ran against were good, but he wanted to push himself, so he put this in his head and it worked. He would tell himself to *go, go, go*, and he became one of the best. He has been doing that ever since. Once he entered the curve, he leaned and started to open up. He was against the clock and he knew it. As John pressed harder, he could feel the pressure, but he continued to press.

"Run John, run harder, harder," yelled Coach Wright and with his team members. They all started to feel good, because it looked as if they were going to win and set a new record in the process. As John came to the line, he almost collapsed from exhaustion.

"We won, John, we won!" yelled his teammates.

"We set a new record," yelled Coach Wright.

The feeling they had was unbelievable. They had done it. They made the Nationals and would run another day. John and his teammates took a victory lap.

When they finished, John found a quiet place to relax and wind down. John's mind at that time focused on the fact that his and Sara's son would have loved to see him run.

Sara's vision appeared and said, "John, don't worry, I am keeping your son abreast on everything you do in life. He will know of you, but he will not meet you until the time is right. He won't know your name, but he will know you." Then her vision faded.

One month later, it was time for the NFL draft. All of the guys on the team had gotten together to go out for a Draft Day Party. They invited all their friends. John was still seeing Sandra, but just as a friend.

"John," said Tony, one of his friends who was a defensive end, and who was also up for the draft. "We may go in the top ten." He and John were both hoping to be picked for the same team.

The draft was held in Ohio. The city was Canton, home of the Pro Football Hall of Fame. John and his teammates were invited to the celebration. You could bring two guests, and John parents went with him.

It was on April twenty-first at twelve noon, but they would have a party the night before. Reporters were all over the place waiting for interviews. This was one of the most nationally-televised events every year.

As everyone took his or her place, the draft begun. Hundreds of players from all parts of the country waited to hear their name. Everyone there was an athlete, but the focus was on the number one player to be picked. No one knew who it would be, but everyone had an idea. The announcer began to call the names out, and everyone knew this would be a long day.

The draft parties around the country were starting to heat up. People went to stadiums and bars, or just stayed at home and grilled, drank, and enjoyed themselves the whole day until the draft was over. Yes, the day had begun, and the clock was ticking for each team as they made their choice.

It went by quickly, and only ten names were left. John didn't know it for sure, but it started to sink in that he may be the number one pick.

The fifth player picked in the draft was Tony Crawford, picked by the Atlanta Bears. John went to congratulate his teammate and friend.

"You made it, man," said John as he hugged his friend. "Now you go make a difference in Atlanta."

"I will," replied Tony, "We still can be in the same league."

"Let's hope so," said John.

Only four names remained, and drum roll was still building. The announcer called out three more names, which took about ten minutes each. John Fields's name didn't come up, so everyone guessed he was going to be next.

Finally, the moment everyone had been waiting had come. Years of working out hard, training in the rain, hot weather, or even cold weather had paid off for these young men and the last name was being called. The announcer's voice spoke, "The number one player is out of Livingston University in North Carolina, Mr. John Fields, by the Dallas Cowboys, who acquired the pick from New England in a trade which took place a couple minutes ago."

After years of work, it finally paid off. John's dream had come true. Everyone hugged him and shook his hand as he took his place on the stage to be given his jersey and hat from Dallas.

Back home, his family was together for a Draft Day party, and boy did they party when his name was called. A family member had made the pros and that was great. That was one day that will never be forgotten. This was one young man who will always be in people's heart and minds.

John called Sandra, and she wished him all the luck in the world. They would always be friends, and they knew this was probably the end of their close friendship.

"I'll miss you, Sandra, but I won't forget you," said John.

Sandra was from Georgia and Dallas places Atlanta in her hometown.

"Maybe you could come to a game?" asked John. "I will get you tickets, just let me know."

"That would be nice," replied Sandra, "but I will have to see where I am. John, it is okay about me and you. You have always been up front and truthful to me. Don't you worry about anything, I will be all right, John. You just find Sara and your son. Good-bye, John Fields," and she hung up the phone.

All that work paid off, now he was going to be the highest paid rookie ever in the history of football. As the party went on into the night, people started to call it a day. The campus where John attended school again returned to the quiet place—or piece of heaven—that God had picked out for them. All across the country the night was silent and the draft would be silent for another year.

A month later, all of John's family attended his graduation. Everyone, students and families, looked so beautiful on this wonderful day. It was one of the largest classes in Livingston's history. As the speaker called out each graduate's name, the audience applauded. The excitement was building and once John's name was called, the crowd gave him a standing ovation for two minutes.

The speaker went on to say, "This young man, in the short period of his life, has been through so much. He is one of the best athletes to come through Livingston. This young man lived through a coma to win athlete of the year. Ladies and gentleman, let's give another hand for Mr. John Fields."

"John, would you like to say a few words?" said the Master of Ceremonies.

"Yes, sir, I would," he replied.

As the words flowed from John's month, the audience was completely silent. They could feel all the emotion in his voice with each word he spoke. John said, "I have enjoyed my teachers and classmates here at Livingston. I've been through a lot, but just being here is like being in a part of heaven, as my GOD watches over us.

"GOD protected me for four years while I was here, and he will be with me when I leave. I thank God for the opportunity to play and attend Livingston. I will miss all of you."

After he finished, John slowly walked to his seat with tears in his eyes. It was the same feeling he had when his grandmother died. That same emptiness, but one thing was a little different, Livingston would always be here. He could come back, he could see the campus and its surroundings, which seemed to make the area look so peaceful. This place he could see in his lifetime. He could only see his grandmother again when he died. He thought about how his grandmother was waiting on him, and he would see her again one day. That day would come and their reunion would be very special.

CHAPTER 8

John returned home before spring camp started. His mother was happy to see him.

"Hi, Son, come on in the house."

John entered through the kitchen because he could smell the food from outside.

"Everyone is waiting, and I made your favorite meal," said his mom.

"Mom, you mean black eye peas, corn, chicken, cornbread and an apple pie?"

"Yes, Honey, I made it all for you on this special day."

"Mom, you're the best, I love you."

When he opened the door to the living room, his family and friends yelled "Surprise!" They were all there to give him a party he would not forget. They had a great time that day. Everyone congratulated and hugged John, for it would be a while before they saw him again. While talking to his friends, everyone asked him to catch a tough pass. John, being the person he was, would say "I will try," and he would.

"I can't tell you how much I really love all of you, and how much all mean to me," said John. "I will miss you, but I will be back every chance I get."

"Now, John," said his mother, "you just enjoy yourself and don't worry, we will all miss you too, but we will come to watch you play."

"Yes, Son," said his dad, "just mail us as many tickets as you can."

They ate, danced, and enjoyed themselves until the sunset. Meanwhile, John slipped away and went down to the woods. He sat on his favorite log. While sitting there, a poem went through his mind. He called it "Log of Thought." John had written this as a sophomore in college. It went,

LOG OF THOUGHT

Hello Lord.
Lord, as I sit here
On this old splintered log,
It starts me to think.
You know I have not talked
To you lately
Everything I ask for
You have given.
My every wish
You have granted.
You've guided my mind
And my tongue in the
Direction they should go.
Yet, I have not thanked you.

>Thank you, Lord
>And Lord, as I sit here
>Being guided through the past
>   and present,
>Thank you for everything,
>Including this old log,
>The Log of Thought."

John's eyes filled with tears, for he had begun to think of Sara and LJ. He lie back on the old log and fell asleep. While sleeping, they came to him in his dreams. They were walking in the woods; it was a beautiful place. The two were laughing and playing.

"Sara, Sara."

"Yes, John. How are you?"

"I am fine, but I need you now more than ever, Sara. If you are real, come to me. Let's be together—the three of us."

"We will, John, soon we will. Our time is near, but you must be patient and let faith lead us."

The blowing wind awakened him and he looked around, not realizing at first it was a dream, because this was his strongest vision ever. A storm was moving in from the east. It was going to be a rough one, and he needed to get out of the woods. The woods were no place to be during a storm. John ran home as fast as he could.

Back home in California, LJ was getting ready to play in the upcoming football season. He was in the eighth grade, but the coaches wanted to put him on the varsity team because he was built for varsity. LJ, like his dad, was on a mission. It was as if he knew they were going to meet. Their paths were closer now than ever.

One night LJ was sitting on the couch watching a Dallas game. John took a hard tackle. LJ felt the pain. Not as strongly as his dad, but he felt it.

"Mom," he said, "I felt that."

"Nonsense," she said. "You mean you felt sorry for the way that guy got hit."

"No Mom, I really felt it—look, here is a bruise."

"Honey, did you fall at school, or get hit during practice?"

"Well, I could have," replied LJ.

After that conversation with his mother, he never told her of any of the pain he felt, but he kept an eye on the man who played for Dallas. His mom could see the things that were happening in his life, and she knew that time was near for him to meet his dad. She knew his dad, but didn't know how to bring them together. Since he's feeling pain, he must be near.

Sara had been seeing John Fields for years: in her dreams and on television. *How can I tell this man he has a son?* she often thought to herself. He had been in her dreams, but she didn't know if she was in his. She thought she was thinking of him just because she loved him. John was thinking the same thing. He thought he was crazy, or just in love.

Their time was getting close, and they would no longer have to feel this way. They could be together if they chose.

LJ had strong feelings as he grew up. He didn't see his dad in visions or anything, but he felt him at times.

All the pain his dad felt, LJ felt also. Not to the extent that John did, but he felt it.

During his high school years, LJ would go to the doctor for aches and pains, but they could not find anything. The doctors just didn't know, and told his mother it could be in his mind, and maybe he should give up sports. "No," said Sara, "that is a decision for him. I will not do this to him. LJ, the doctor thinks this is in your head and you should give up sports. What do you wish to do son?"

"Mom, if it's in my head, why do I feel pain? That means that it can happen for the rest of my life."

"Yes honey, but maybe not," said Sara.

"I wish to keep playing because I love the game, and I can't quit now. I feel as if I have to play. Do you know what I am saying?" said LJ. "I feel as if I am on a mission, but I don't know what for yet."

"When the time is right, you will," replied Sara. "You will. Dear, I feel the same thing. I want you to do whatever you wish; I will support you," she added.

So, when his senior year came around, he had played in every game, but LJ still felt a little pain from time to time.

LJ grew up fast. He was a senior in high school, and doing well in everything he did, but football was his sport. Although he complained about his knee hurting, the doctors couldn't find anything wrong, so he played with a little pain all year. Meanwhile, his dad had injured his knee, and that was the pain LJ was feeling. John had played five years for Dallas, but he had to sit out a season because of that injury.

LJ graduated from high school and received honors, just like his parents had. He wished his dad could see him play one game while he was in high school. He had no idea it would come true.

He was one of the top high school players in the country. California gave LJ the top high school football player award as the number. one player in the state. He was also picked to play in the senior's last game. In a few weeks, East and West seniors were scheduled to play each other in a yearly meeting which dated back fifty-five years. The seniors really got a chance to show off their talent to college scouts. Some had already committed to schools.

It was like an alumni meeting, all the greats were there. LJ, like all the other boys, was hoping to go out with a "bang." West team was the favorite, although East had won the last two years in a row.

One-half hour before the game started, the bands that were invited put on a beautiful opening show. All the people in the stands were so excited because it was not even half time.

The alumni players got a chance to march onto the field, and as they did each of their names were called out. John Fields met John Jessie Hart for the first time. He met his son and he was not aware of the connection, neither was LJ aware that John was his father. It was a feeling that touched both of them. They both felt something special. Yes, destiny was at work as they stopped in front of each other to say hello.

"Hello, Mr. Fields," said LJ. "You are the best."

"Thank you very much young man, but I have heard of you and you're still in high school. That is very impressive. Excuse me," said John. "Do I know you?"

LJ responded, "No, sir, I don't think you do."

"Where are you from?" said John Fields.

"California, my family is from there," replied LJ. "They have lived there all my life."

"I knew this lady..." and before John could finish his sentence, they were disturbed.

"LJ," yelled the coach. "Let's go, son."

"Well, sir, I have to go," and he shook John Fields hand.

Afterwards, just like that, LJ was gone. Just like Sara, when John first met her. Only the feeling he felt was not one of loneliness like with Sara. He knew there was something special about this kid. But what was it? he wondered.

The game was set to begin as the bands left the field. The East kicked off to the West, who put on a great drive to score and took a seven-to-nothing lead. Then it was the East's turn to get the ball. The West team's kicker placed the ball deep in the end zone, and East couldn't bring it out. The East had a great running back, but on their first drive couldn't put anything together and was forced to punt the ball.

The first quarter ran out with the score the same, seven to zero in favor of the West. As West received the punt in the second quarter they tried a reverse, but the East stopped them on their own ten yard line. On West's first play the halfback fumbled the ball, and a lineman from the East covered it at the seven.

East took possession of the ball, and two plays later took it in for a score. Steve Marshall, a back from Fort Mont, Texas, carried it in. With the score now seven to seven, East kicked off to the West. The time was winding down in the first half. Three minutes to go, and LJ intercepted a ball and took it thirty yards for a score. Leading fourteen to seven, the West kicked off to the East with one minute and thirty seconds left in the first half of a great game.

East surprised West with a great wall set up by the lineman on the kickoff team, which saw their return man, Calvin Muffin, take it eighty yards and score to tie the game up at fourteen. East kicked off again, but West could not do anything before time ran out in the first half.

Both teams went into their locker rooms as the first half came to a close.

"LJ, we have got to make something happen on defense," the coach said. LJ was one of the captains on defense.

As the bands lit up the field, both teams got ready for what was going to be a great finish.

"Listen up," said the coach. "I want all of you to play hard and just do your jobs. Win or lose, it is not that important, it's how you play the game that they will remember the most. Now let's get pumped up. Pump them up, LJ."

LJ led the cheers.

"Who are we?"

"West coast champs."

"Who are we?"

"West coast champs."

"What we gonna do?"

"Score, score, score. Go west coast!" and the team went back out onto the field.

The second half began. The game was shaping up to be the best battle the East and West teams had ever had. Midway through the third quarter they really started to test LJ, but penalties slowed East's attack. LJ and the defensive backs had really been tested. On one play series in the third quarter, the East through three of six balls on LJ's side of the field, but penalties slowed their attack. They were hit with an illegal block in the back, which put LJ on this sidelines for the rest of the quarter. As he got hit, his dad could feel it, and he jumped to his feet to see if the young man was okay. He was fine as they walked him off.

But it still did not come that easy. The East was ready to play. They always turned out some good, young talent, and it showed. While through the third and fourth quarter each team scored a pair of touchdowns, both coaches knew their defensive teams would have to step up. Everyone in the stands was exhausted from cheering so much.

The East and West played one of the best games in the history of the contest.

With six minutes to go, LJ got ready to go back into the game. His mom and dad were happy to see this. LJ's granddad paid him a visit on the sidelines while he was getting ready.

"Son."

"Yes, granddad?"

"I am proud of you, and so is your mom. Are you okay? Remember when you were young, and the defense needed to get a score for their team to win?"

"Yes," said LJ.

"Well, it is like that again. You've seen what the quarterback is doing during the whole game, now go out and do what you have to do. You can do it, you can do it, son."

With that in mind, LJ went out on a mission. "Let's go, defense!" he called out as they formed a circle around him. He was the captain and he called the formations.

On the East's forty yard line, it was third down and ten. LJ knew it was time to pass. "Pass, pass, pass," he yelled, and the defense shifted to cover the flanks. Sure enough, it was a pass. With a minute and forty-five seconds left in the game, LJ picked off the ball and was going to score.

Sara's dad ran out of his seat and down the sideline, just like when LJ was a little boy. "Run, son, run," he yelled. It was one of the most special moments you had ever seen. Mr. Moright was up there in age, but he ran all the way. When he returned to his seat, he said to Sara, "Honey, I am too old for this. Let's go home."

John could only sit and look as the East team lost the game on a last-minute play by a young man who would definitely be in the pros one day. He only wished that Dallas would get him first.

LJ thought about the man he met at the game. He told his mom about him, and she said, "We need to try and find your dad soon. Son, we both miss him, and want him in our lives. We have waited long enough. LJ, there is something I must tell you."

"Everyone to the showers," yelled the coach as LJ was trying to answer his mom.

"We'll talk later, Mom," he said, and was off to the locker room.

Over the next four years John was busy playing in the pros and LJ was going through college. During this time Sara's mother died, and John felt the pain. He appeared, to let her know that he was there for her. "Sara, I feel your pain, and I also have pain. When you cry I cry also. GOD will heal your pain if you let him and you will be ok. I love you and miss not being there, but you will always be in my heart." Then his vision faded.

Sara's brother, Wiliam, had joined the Naval Academy and graduated to become a commissioned officer in the U.S. Navy.

LJ's years in school went as planned, and he excelled in sports just like his dad. Yes, their faith was closer now than ever, and they knew this.

John's friend, Tony Crawford, was killed in a private plane while flying back to North Carolina to visit a sick relative. He was still playing with the Atlanta team. John attended his funeral, which was held in Kannapolis, North Carolina, where he was born. Then John returned to Dallas to get ready for his ninth year as a pro. He kept up with the young man who he had met at the East/West game. When the young man graduated, John knew it, and knew where he was going. He would have to play him soon. Their faith was closer now than ever.

LJ graduated from college and was picked by the San Francisco Bears as their number one draft choice. He married a classmate whom he had dated since their freshman year. She was from Denver. That first season he would play against his dad—the man he had met at the East/West game. Although LJ didn't know for certain that this man was his dad, he could feel that this was a very special person in his life.

The season began, and Dallas Cowboys were scheduled to meet San Francisco in the sixth game of the season, in San Francisco. John, hurt again for the second time in his career, watched from the sidelines as LJ stole the show. He picked off three balls and scored on one. San Francisco won the game. During the game, LJ felt something strange every time he looked at John. John felt strange also when he looked at LJ.

During one play LJ got hit hard. John felt the pain, not as bad as LJ felt it, but pain. He jumped to his feet. LJ was okay. After the game, they saw each other in the distance. It was as if they each knew what the other was thinking.

"Goodbye, Mr. Fields."

"Goodbye, John Hart."

Then they both turned and left the field.

"Mom, I saw that man who plays with Dallas again, I wish we could talk to him. He is one of the best receivers in the league. I feel strange when I am around him."

"LJ, I tried to talk to you before about your dad."

"Yes mom," said LJ with excitement in his voice.

Sara went on to say. "I've seen him in my dreams, but I can't say if Mr. Fields is your father. Your father knows you, I feel, but he doesn't know your name or how you look either. I know the area where we lived in North Carolina. We will go there after you play in Dallas."

"Okay, Mom, that will be great because I feel it is time to meet this man."

As they hugged each other they both began to cry because it was time for them to meet faith.

John was crying also as he sat in his car after the game. He was feeling what Sara and LJ were feeling, and as he tried to hold back the tears he couldn't. He just missed the boy he met and could feel something special for him. He also was thinking about the dreams he had of a son, and wished he were like this young man.

The next game was set for December twelfth and John was ready to play. Even though it was his ninth year as a pro, he was still the best around.

They played in Texas, and San Francisco had not

played well there over the past five years. On game day everyone was set for one of the best games ever. The number one veteran was taking on the number one rookie in the league. The number one defensive player of Dallas was taking on the number one offensive player of San Francisco. Yes, this was the day a lot of people had waited for.

Both teams took their turns running out onto the field while the crowds cheered them on. San Francisco was the first out because they were the visiting team. Then Dallas came out, and the sounds of cannon fire echoed through the air.

"Are you ready?" The Dallas coach asked John.

"Sure, Coach, I feel great," John replied.

"Good," said the coach, "we need you to step up strong today and be the leader you are."

"Coach, I will, I will," said John.

"The last time that rookie picked off three balls, one for a score," said coach Ward in an angry voice.

"I will chew that rookie up and spit him out like bad food," replied John.

Meanwhile, LJ was warming up when his coach began talking to him also.

"Are you okay?" asked Coach Jones.

"Yeah, but I feel a little strange."

"Strange?" asked the coach.

"Yeah, I can't explain it, but I am ready to play. I am just nervous I guess, Coach," LJ said.

"Well," said the coach, "that is natural."

"You will have to play the best receiver in the league as a rookie. That doesn't happen too often, but we know you can handle the job, LJ."

"John Fields, I know a lot about him, I used to watch him play when I was growing up. He is the best—even at his age."

"That's what I was going to tell you," said the coach.

"LJ, you're very smart, and that's why you're starting as a rookie. Don't let the age fool you, and don't take him for granted, because that's where people mess up and he scores."

"Thanks, Coach, I will do my best."

CHAPTER 9

It was game day in Dallas, Texas. The team captains met for the coin toss. Dallas chose tails. Tails it was, and Dallas would receive the ball as the game began. As both teams lined up for the kick-off, electricity filled the air. It was Sunday afternoon, and a lovely day, and there were sixty thousand people screaming for their team. Yet, when the referee blew his whistle, it was as if no one made a single sound.

The kicker placed the ball deep into the end zone and Zack Anthony brought it out. He started up the middle for about twenty yards, but his blocking broke down so he took it to the outside and got a nice gain to the thirty-five yard line before being tackled.

"Nice, Zack!" yelled the coach.

"Offense, hit the field," said Coach Henry. "Listen, Marshall," the coach said to the quarterback, "this is the play out I want run."

The first play was a pitch to the outside, which gained

six yards. Second down and four on their own forty-one yard line, they ran a play up the middle for two yards on a fullback dive. At third down and two yards to go for the first down, Dallas was stopped and forced to punt.

The first half of the game Dallas chose to stay away from the rookie. On one play in the first quarter, they tested him. The ball was on Dallas's forty yard line and they needed ten yards to keep the drive alive. Slot right, flanker would go in motion to the right, and then the tight end would go down and they would cross to mix up the defenders. But LJ and the safety broke it up. LJ almost picked it off. The ball came to the outside and he was there. "Man, I had that one," he said, then yelled to the rookie, "Yes sir, and come back my way; just come back." That was the last time they tried that play in the first half. But the second half would be a different story.

At halftime the score was 0–0. Both locker rooms were quiet. John was talking to one of the assistant coaches. "Are we going to attack the rookie?"

"Yeah, this half we will see how tough he is," the coach replied.

Meanwhile, in San Francisco's locker room, they were talking about the same thing. "LJ, you know they will try you the second half," said the coach. "It's the only thing they have left so be ready."

"I will, Coach, I will."

As both teams came out for the second half, LJ sat behind for a second. John did the same thing. It was as if they knew what the other was thinking. John was thinking *I have to catch a pass over that rookie.* LJ thinking, *I have to be ready, I know who is going to try and get open.*

At the same time, John commented, "God bless the rookie."

LJ said, "God bless the old man." They could almost hear each other.

The second half began and Dallas kicked off. LJ received the kick-off and brought it out to the fifty yard line. It was beautiful to see a rookie run like that. John could only watch. He started out years ago running back kick-offs. Once in the league, he proved to be one of the best. As LJ was hit on the fifty yard line the ball came loose, but he was out of bounds. John could feel the pain in his left arm. He looked to see if LJ was okay. He was all right. *Why do I feel pain whenever he gets hit?* John thought, *but then again, maybe I am just hoping the rookie doesn't get hurt.*

There was something strange about that young man, but John couldn't figure it out. *Why do I feel his pain at times? Why do I feel as if I know him? I need to talk to him again.* John couldn't figure it out because LJ's last name was not the same as his mother's. Yes, LJ's grandfather was smart; he had given him a different last name so John wouldn't know him.

LJ got up and looked at John. It was as if to say "I'm fine." John shook his head at the rookie. In a way to say, "Yes." He said, "That's my boy, yes, that's my boy."

Both teams had a tough defense and they were living up to it tonight. Both teams had only managed a field goal thus far. Tied at three, San Franscio started the fourth quarter with the ball.

Running a very good mixture of plays, they managed to put a drive together, but due to penalties had to kick another field goal. With the score now six–three, time was running out. Dallas really needed to put a series together in order to win.

With five minutes left on the clock, John got his first catch of the day. He went into motion and came across the middle. Dallas was moving the ball now and seemed confident. On the twenty yard line of San Francisco, a pass play again was called. John was the one the play was set up for.

"Down, set, hut one!" John Fields went into motion. It was a way to get him away from the rookie. On this particular play, LJ went with him. As John came out, LJ got picked hard. He was knocked down and out of his covering of John.

John, meanwhile, came across the middle and went up for the ball. Caught in an awkward position, he got hit hard also. As John got hit, LJ screamed out "No!" for he felt the pain. As John hit the ground, he was knocked out. LJ got up and ran to him. John was out cold.

They had to bring the stretcher out on the field after the doctor checked him out. The doctor believed it to be a neck and spinal injury. LJ was in tears as he ran toward his mom and his wife.

"When that man got hit, I felt the pain. I *really* felt pain, all these things are just too strange about him."

"I felt the pain as well," replied his Mom. "We really should go to the hospital to see him. Son, you're right, this John Fields may be your dad."

LJ, his wife, Melody, and Sara, with tears in their eyes, left the stadium without waiting for the game to end and drove to the nearby hospital. They didn't say a word, but LJ and Sara both felt the pain of what John Fields was going through.

CHAPTER 10

Sara, LJ, and Melody arrived at the hospital. As they entered and stopped at the front desk, John's teammates and family were in the lobby. The nurse pointed out Mrs. Fields. Sara approached her and asked how John was doing.

"The doctor said he is in a coma," Mrs. Fields said, "and they will have to operate. Do I know you?" she asked Sara and LJ.

"No, you don't, but we are friends of your son and we want to make sure that he's okay."

"Well, I am glad that you came. Everyone here is like family," said Mrs. Fields.

John's mother really didn't know Sara. They had never met before, and little did she know that soon she would meet her grandson.

"Come in, and have a seat with me over here," said Mrs. Fields.

LJ's eyes filled with tears as he thought about the man

who may be his dad. They would not let anyone see John because he was in a coma, so LJ, Melody, and Sara had a seat with the rest of the family.

After hours of sitting, LJ had fallen asleep. While sleeping, he dreamed about his dad. He was walking on a football field, and it was cloudy, with a mist in the air. As he crossed the field, he saw a man lying face down. His face was coming clear, and LJ began to run toward him.

"Dad, Dad, it's me, your son."

As LJ got closer to the man, he saw that he wasn't moving, but lying in a still position. He looked as if he was asleep, but it was a deep sleep.

"Dad, Dad, wake up, I need you. Mom has told me so much about you and I want to know you. Wake up, please? God, please wake him up and let him live. Just tell him to open his eyes."

Not getting a response, LJ turned slowly and started to walk away with even more tears streaming down his face. As he began to leave the field, John slowly opened his eyes.

"Son, Son, it's okay. I am okay, don't cry. Tell them I am all right. Tell your mother I love the both of you. Thanks, Son, for coming to me."

The dream, which seem so real, was over. LJ woke up feeling strange. He looked at his mom and Mrs. Fields, who were engaged in a conversation near his chair.

"Mrs. Fields, Mom, John is awake now."

"Excuse me?" said Mrs. Fields.

"He said to tell you he would be okay."

Mrs. Fields said, "No, young man, my son is in a coma.

You had a dream and it's good that it was positive about him."

"He is fine and he said he was hungry," said LJ.

About that time, the doctor came out of John's room.

"Mr. And Mrs. Fields, I don't know what to say."

"What do you mean doctor?" replied Mrs. Fields.

"Is my son okay?" Mr. Fields asked.

"Yes, he is fine. He just woke up, and the first thing he said was that he is hungry."

"That's my son," said Mrs. Fields.

Everyone turned and looked at LJ. Mrs. Fields said, "I don't know who you are, but GOD works through you as he does through my son. He has been able to do things like you just did all his life."

"May we see him?" asked Mrs. Fields.

"Yes, you can, but make it short. He needs to rest," replied the doctor.

Sara and LJ decided to leave and come back another day. "Mrs. Fields, me and my son will be back later, when John has rested."

"Who are you again?" said Mrs. Fields.

"I'm Sara Moright, and this is my son, John. We are glad that your son is going to be okay."

"Well, I thank God for you, please come back," said Mrs. Fields.

Then Mrs. Fields gave LJ a hug like John's grandfather used to do. "I don't know why it seems as if I know you, you feel like family," said Mrs. Fields, "and I love you both."

Sara and LJ checked into a nearby motel. Sara, wishing to be alone, took a walk to the woods. She didn't know how to tell John he had a son. While in the woods. John's image appeared.

"Hello, Sara. Sara, I am fine and would like to meet my son. Sara I love you."

"John, I love you also, and I am glad God took care of you."

"Please come and see me soon. We have a lot of catching up to do."

Just like that, the vision was gone. Sara now had the strength to go and see her long lost love.

LJ and his mother waited for three days and finally they were able to see John. Once they arrived at the hospital, John could feel their presence. His room was so crowded with people. People were laughing and talking to each other.

"Are you okay, John?" asked one of his brothers.

"Yes, I just feel something wonderful coming my way. Excuse me," said John. "Would everyone please stand over on this side of the room?"

Larry said to his wife, "Honey, he's starting to act weird again. Remember when he got up sleep walking and blowing like he was crazy?"

"Yes," replied Rebecca.

"Well," said Mr. Fields, "he has that same look in his eyes."

"John, John, are you okay, son?" asked his mom.

John just stared at the door.

"Why is he looking at the door," asked Larry.

About that time, Sara, Melody, and LJ walked into the room. John and Sara's eyes met again like the first time. It was as if no one was there but the two of them. As Sara walked further into the room, the magic was the same as when they looked at each other for the first time years ago.

Both were calling each other's name at the same time. They were excited and crying as they embraced each other, even as John still lay in bed. It seemed as if it was the first time again.

"John," said Sara. I want you to meet someone special. John, this is your son."

Everyone in the room started to murmur, when Mrs. Fields walked up.

"With all the excitement in the world in her voice, she said, "What? I have a grandson? I have a grandson, and a beautiful daughter!" then she hugged them both with tears in her eyes.

"Hello, Grandmother and this is my wife, Melody," said LJ. Mrs. Fields was so happy she didn't know what to do. LJ's wife was expecting a child in about six months also.

Mrs. Fields said, "Years ago, John had a dream where he was walking and breathing, you must be that dream he had."

"I have had dreams all my life and I didn't understand them," John said. "Now I do, now I do. I have a son. I have a son!" As they hugged each other, it was the most wonderful feeling they both had ever felt.

"Son!"

"Dad! I love you dad."

"I love you son."

Everyone in the hospital room was shocked. They could only cry because the excitement was so great. John's brother and sisters were the most excited. They hugged Sara and her son and didn't want to let go.

"Now, let's get out of here," said Mrs. Fields. "So he can get some rest."

"Wait, Mom," said John. "With all the excitement I forgot to ask one question. What is your name, son?"

"My name is John Jessie Hart, but they call me LJ for short."

Both John and Sara were so excited they forgot that part.

"Well, you come with me," Mrs. Fields said to LJ.

As everyone left the room, John held Sara's hand and would not let go.

"Hello, my Butterfly."

"Hello, my Sunshine."

"I love you, lady, and I missed you so much. I have never stopped loving you."

"John, I have never stopped loving you either."

As they looked at each other the magic was still there, just as when they first met. "You get some rest and we will be waiting for you," Sara said.

"I have a son, I have a son," John said, and closed his eyes and started to rest as Sara rubbed his head lightly.

John left the hospital after about a week. Sara and LJ were waiting. After meeting the family members and talking with his parents, John decided to take his long lost love and his son to the woods for a walk. They were to be a family now, after all these years of dreaming and praying.

They all walked down one of the paths that led to their special place. LJ and his wife walked down another path, once it split off.

John was walking and holding Sara's hand as he said to her, "I never stopped loving you, and I don't ever want you to leave me again."

"John, I have waited so long to find you," replied Sara, "and I wouldn't think of leaving if you want me to stay. As for your son, you couldn't talk him away if you tried."

Once they arrived at their special place in the woods, John and Sara noticed that things looked different. The stream was still there, but it did not have that magical zest about it. The little creatures that had enriched it were all but gone, and the stream was lifeless but still flowing well.

As John and LJ traveled separate paths to the center of the woods, they met at a big oak tree that had been there for years. John and Sara had carved their names in it.

"You look on that side, Son, and I will look over here."

"I found it, Dad, I found it right here."

You could barely see their names because the tree had grown a lot.

"Mom, that is so cool, you and Dad did this."

"Yes, Son," said his mom, "we were young and in love."

"Love makes you do weird things," said LJ.

"Honey, I still love you the same," said John. "Now let's put our new initials on this tree."

"What do you mean, John?" asked Sara.

"Sara, will you marry me?"

Sara started to cry because the man she had loved all her life still loved her. "Yes, I will, yes I will, John."

LJ was crying also, because the man he had heard so much about was for real and just as he imagined. Yes, they were about to become a family.

The wind started to blow very gently, John felt that it was his grandmother congratulating him and telling him she was happy.

"Now you and your son take a walk and get to know each other," Sara said.

Sara and Melody sat down on a bench that had been added to the woods to help beautify it as John walked off with his son. About that time a squirrel hurried up a tree near where they walked. As the squirrel looked down at the people below, he felt there was no danger and came back down toward LJ. The little creature kept coming toward LJ as if it had met him before.

LJ found an acorn and placed in his open right hand. The squirrel took it out of his palm, ran up the tree, and sat on a limb that stretched out over the creek. John could only look with amazement, and think, *that's my son*.

John said, "You know, Son, I had the moves on you in that game, but the quarterback just couldn't get the ball to me."

"Dad, no way, I had you covered like two slices of bread. Just like this—you're the ham in the middle."

As he bumped his dad, John yelled out with pain.

"Dad, Dad. You okay?"

"Psych," said his dad.

Then John reached his arms up as if he were catching a pass. "Touchdown," he yelled out. "You see, Son, I would have scored. Son. I love you."

"Dad, I love you also."

They walked back toward Sara. "Butterfly?" John said.

"Yes, Sunshine?" said Sara.

"Let's go home," said John.

They walked off into the night, admiring the beautiful stars and talking about life.

LJ commented, "Dad, I always wanted a sister."

"Well, we will have to talk that over with Mom."

"Honey, when you get well we will talk about that," said Sara.

"I have dreamed about twins and thought that it would be nice if we get blessed with them," replied John.

"Maybe we will have twin grandchildren," Sara said to LJ.

"So, it looks like our plan to be together in life worked out after all," said John.

"Our faith," replied Sara, "faith."

As they all walked back to the house, at the same time John and Sara said, "Thank you, Lord, for faith."

At last the night was silent and the town was at rest.

Silent Dreams was designed and typeset in Bell by Kachergis Book Design of Pittsboro, North Carolina. It was printed and bound by Edwards Brothers of Ann Arbor, Michigan.